The London Murder Mysteries

Cora Harrison is the author of many successful books for children and adults, including the *Drumshee* series set in Ireland. She lives on a small farm in the west of Ireland with her husband, her German Shepherd dog called Oscar and a very small white cat called Polly.

Find out more about Cora at:
www.coraharrison.com

To discover why Cora wrote
the London Murder Mysteries, head online to:
piccadillypress.co.uk/londonmurdermysteries

The London Murder Mysteries

The Montgomery Murder
The Deadly Fire
Murder on Stage
Death of a Chimney Sweep (Coming Soon)

THE LONDON MURDER MYSTERIES

MURDER ON STAGE

CORA HARRISON

PICCADILLY PRESS • LONDON

*This book is dedicated to Cath Thompson,
my dear friend and former colleague, who,
over and above the call of duty, has read and
commented on my dozens of books.
I hope she will enjoy this story
about her beloved 'Garden'.*

First published in Great Britain in 2011
by Piccadilly Press Ltd,
5 Castle Road, London NW1 8PR
www.piccadillypress.co.uk

Text copyright © Cora Harrison, 2011

A catalogue record for this book is available
from the British Library

ISBN: 978 1 84812 111 9 (paperback)

3 5 7 9 10 8 6 4 2

Printed in the UK by CPI Bookmarque, Croydon, CR0 4TD
Cover design by Patrick Knowles
Cover illustration by Chris King

CHAPTER 1

POISON

Only Alfie saw the hand. He stared in horror, opened his mouth, but then shut it again. With all the noise going on in the theatre, the whistles, shouts, screams, catcalls, no one would hear him.

Alfie, his brother Sammy, their cousins Jack and Tom and their friend Sarah were standing right in front of the stage at Covent Garden Theatre. A man had given Alfie a sheaf of tickets, telling him to bring his friends and make as much noise as possible when the signal was given, and promising him a shilling later. It was a great occasion for a riot. The Queen herself, the young Queen Victoria, was present!

All was quiet until an actor came on stage to announce the next play – Alfie recognised him as Harry Booth. This was the sign for the rioting to begin. Someone shouted from the gallery, a man leant over the balcony rail and yelled down to the pit. A woman from down there screamed back. Two men in the pit hurled oranges up towards the gallery, where Alfie saw them burst with a mess of juice and pulp. 'Old prices! Old prices! Old prices!' they all bellowed.

Everyone had turned around to watch the rioters. No one was looking at the man on stage and his words were drowned by the din. Alfie looked up, laughed at the dummy of the theatre manager, with a rope around his cloth neck, being lowered from the rails of the gallery. Then he looked back at the stage – and saw the hand.

The hand came slowly and cautiously out from the place where the two curtains joined, just behind where a small table with a glass stood. It grasped a glass phial in its fist. Alfie could see the sleeve and the top of the phial gleaming in the white glow from the gas-fired limelights on the edge of the stage. He watched intently as the liquid from the phial was poured into the glass.

Harry Booth finished his speech, bowed to an

audience who had not heard a word he had said, and picked up the glass – a glass of port it looked like . . .

Instantly Alfie acted.

In a moment he had scaled the small wooden barrier between the orchestra and the audience and was pushing his way past the conductor, the violinists, the flute players and the drummers.

He knew where he was going.

During the long and boring opera that had gone before he had seen how to get on the stage from the pit. An actor, dressed as the devil, had slipped into the orchestra pit and then risen up as if by magic right in the middle of the stage.

Where he had gone, Alfie could follow.

Yes, there was a trapdoor. The bright, white light from the stage outlined it. Alfie pushed and in a moment he had swung himself up.

It was too late!

Harry Booth was lying dead on the stage.

Instantly Alfie made up his mind. There was nothing he could do. He had not been in time to prevent the murder so now he must get off the stage.

Ever since the death of his parents, Alfie had lived on the edge of danger as well of starvation, and had learnt to bolt for home when trouble arose. He took one look at the audience – still turned away from the stage – and one last look at the body.

Already a man had dashed out from behind the stage and was kneeling beside the body as Alfie hastily retreated back down through the trapdoor. He slid past the musicians who were still playing, and slipped quietly back over the barrier.

Sarah and Jack, only a few months younger than himself, were both on the alert. Sarah was clever. Her eyes would have followed Alfie. Already she had moved forward, and so had Jack, his left hand firmly clasping Sammy's arm. Alfie jerked his head. Jack would guide the blind boy and young Tom would follow after. Moving quietly along, step by careful step, keeping in the shadow of the stage above, Alfie led the way to the exit.

'Let's get out of here,' he said when the others joined him. 'There's going to be trouble. The geezer is dead.'

CHAPTER 2

MURDER

Alfie, Sammy and their cousins had their home in a small, damp cellar in Bow Street, not far from Covent Garden market. When Alfie's parents died, he took over the responsibilities of finding the weekly rent and feeding the four of them. He had promised his dying mother that he would look after his blind brother and that meant that he had to keep a roof over their heads.

The boys begged, stole, performed tricks and Sammy, who had a voice like an angel, could always earn some money from his singing. Sarah lived at a big house where she was a scullery maid but she often visited the boys when she had finished work. That evening, Alfie, with a bundle of free tickets in his pocket, had grandly invited her to go to the theatre with them.

As soon as they started to go down the steps, they heard an excited bark and once Alfie had opened the door, a large and very hairy dog threw himself at them. Mutsy was no beauty. He was a big dog, with masses of reddish brown fur, a fringe hanging over his eyes and enormous paws.

'No sausages today, boy.' Alfie patted the dog. He frowned slightly as they entered. There wasn't much light in the cellar, but it was enough to show that there was nothing to eat.

Tom made a disgusted sound. 'Waste of time!' he said. 'Why did you rush away like that? You should have got some money from that fellow. What was the point of going there for nothing? Just boring, it was!'

'He promised us a shilling, but I wasn't going to wait around. Not with Harry Booth dead on the stage,' said Alfie briefly. He was annoyed with himself for not demanding money first, but that was none of Tom's business. Alfie was the gang leader and that was the way it was going to stay. He opened his mouth to say something angry, but then shut it firmly. Eleven-year-old Tom was a nuisance, always complaining about something, but there was no sense in starting a fight.

'Funny, though, wasn't it? Do you think that he had loads of tickets, then?' asked Sarah. 'These things cost money. I've seen the prices written up. You pay a guinea for a box, fourteen shillings and sixpence for the stalls, six shillings for the pit and four shillings for the upper gallery.'

'Six shillings!' exclaimed Tom. 'For that!'

Alfie frowned. It did seem strange. 'We didn't have seats,' he pointed out. 'Perhaps it's only a few pence if you're standing.'

'What was he like, the bloke that gave you the tickets?' asked Tom.

'Don't remember him too well,' said Alfie reluctantly. 'Small fellow – small and fat. Came up to me when I was doing a spot of juggling. Funny voice – a bit squeaky, like.'

'Stupid!' exclaimed Tom. 'Why didn't you look at him, proper? Then you could have chased him up for the shilling.'

'Who are you calling stupid?' demanded Alfie.

'What actually happened on the stage?' asked Sammy. Though younger than Tom, he had more brains in his little finger than Tom had in his whole body.

Being blind made him extra-sensitive to voices: he sensed his brother's discomfiture and annoyance and now he sat down beside the fire, put his arm around Mutsy and turned his sightless eyes towards Alfie.

'It was really strange.' Alfie sat beside him and Mutsy wagged his tail and sat back on his hindquarters, placing a large hairy paw on each boy's lap. Jack put a few more coals on the fire. He was the one that would have to fish some pieces of coal out of the icy waters of the Thames next morning, but no food meant that the fire was needed more than ever – an empty belly made you shiver – that was the experience of the gang. Alfie gave him a nod of thanks and continued with his story, relating how he had seen the hand pour something from a phial into the glass and how he had dashed on to the stage to try to prevent Harry Booth drinking whatever had been put in the glass.

'Whatever it was, it killed him instant,' he finished, conscious that his stomach was aching with hunger and wishing that, like Mutsy, he liked rats. There were more of them around than there was food – if you were poor that was. If you were rich, the shops and public houses and eating places were full of delicious dishes.

'Any way of finding out who killed him, Alfie?'

Sammy had a quiet smile on his face. 'I was just thinking that Inspector Denham might be interested. Might give us a shilling or two if we could help.'

It was true that Inspector Denham had rewarded them well in the past when the sharp wits of the gang had led to the solution of a crime. Alfie licked the corners of his lips as the saliva began to flow at the thought of the wonderful meals that they had got with Inspector Denham's money.

'Did you see his face?' asked Jack, but Alfie shook his head.

'No, just the arm,' he said. 'Something funny about it, though . . .'

And then his mind went back to that moment at the theatre and suddenly he knew the truth.

The arm had a fancy sleeve – like a clown's costume.

'It was a clown,' he said excitedly. 'I'd bet anything that it was one of the clowns. The sleeve had that frilly end on it – just like the clowns have.'

'Why should a clown murder an actor?' Tom sounded scornful.

'A clown is a man,' pointed out Sarah. 'He could have a reason for murder, same as anyone. And, what's more, it would make a good disguise, what with all that paint on the face and those fancy clothes. It would be hard to know your own brother if he were dressed up as a clown,' she added slowly, thinking her way through the problem.

'And there's clowns coming out of your ears around here since they put that sign up,' said Alfie. He had seen a queue a mile long at the back of the theatre that very morning, behind a board saying:

CLOWNS WANTED:
TEN NEW CLOWNS ON STAGE
EVERY NIGHT,
A SHILLING A NIGHT PAID.

And that was on top of the two regular clowns at Covent Garden Theatre.

'So it could be any of them,' Jack said.

'We have to look for someone who wanted Harry Booth dead.' Alfie was finding that thinking about the murder reduced the terrible ache of hunger. He would keep his mind on that problem.

'Someone who wanted his job,' suggested Tom.

'Not likely,' said Alfie and then changed it quickly to, 'but it's possible.' He didn't want Tom going into one of his sulks.

'He might have injured someone once,' said Sarah.

'Or he might know something about someone,

threatened him, like.' Sammy was enjoying himself, Alfie knew by the look on his brother's face. He had a sharp brain and loved to use it.

'Might have been a blackmailer, mightn't he? What was Harry Booth like, Jack? You said that you and Alfie met him,' said Sarah.

'He was all right – a nice fellow – gave us a few pence for helping him to shift some of these big picture things that they put up at the back of the stage – scenery, that's it. What did you think of him, Alfie?'

Alfie thought. He had no very strong impression of Harry Booth, though he had recognised him instantly each time that he came on stage – not a particularly good actor – he was the same in every one of the small parts that he played.

'He was all right,' he said in the end. It was strange, he thought, a bit sad perhaps – but Harry Booth dead seemed more interesting than Harry Booth alive. 'I'll go down to Covent Garden Theatre tomorrow afternoon and do a bit of poking around,' he went on. 'They're bound to need someone to do a bit of cleaning up. Them tomatoes and oranges didn't half make a mess.'

Who had murdered Harry Booth? Was it one of the theatre's two permanent clowns, or one of the ten who came for one night's performance and might never be seen again?

Whoever it was, they arrived at the theatre well prepared for the deed. Some fast-acting poison had been poured into that glass; Harry Booth had died within seconds of drinking it.

A murderer with a poison like that in his pocket was a very dangerous man!

CHAPTER 3

WANTED!

It had been a frustrating morning for Alfie and Tom.

They had hoped to get some work at the butcher's shop. Sometimes he wanted help in sweeping and scrubbing and was willing to give a few pounds of sausages in return for a couple of hours' work. He was a friendly fellow, and took an interest in the four orphan boys from the cellar near to his shop. But the heavy, thick fog meant that there were few customers and the butcher preferred to do his own sweeping rather than stand around shivering.

When the bells from St Martin's church sounded, Alfie decided it was time for them to go home. But when they reached the pavement by the steps to the cellar, Alfie stopped in horror.

A large poster was pasted to the lamp-post opposite the boys' home. Alfie stared at it for several seconds.

'What's that?' asked Tom. Tom couldn't read, but Alfie could.

And he almost wished that he had never learnt.

In huge letters at the top were the words:

SCOTLAND YARD.
THE COVENT GARDEN THEATRE
MURDER

And underneath this in letters just as large were the words:

WANTED ON SUSPICION OF MURDER
A BOY AGED ABOUT TWELVE
WEARING A CAP AND A TORN JACKET
LAST SEEN YESTERDAY ON STAGE
AT COVENT GARDEN THEATRE.

'Let's get out of here,' muttered Alfie. He hurtled down the steps, twisted the key in the lock, dived in and then slammed the door behind him.

'What's wrong?' asked Tom.

'Scotland Yard,' said Alfie briefly. He wished that Tom would shut up and let him think, but Tom never gave up so he explained hastily. 'They're the high-up police – they'd be more important than the lot at Bow Street Police Station – more important than Inspector Denham, himself. And they're after me. I've been seen, seen on the stage beside a dead man. I'm wanted for murder!'

'What!'

The sight of Tom with his mouth open and his eyes full of terror calmed Alfie.

'Nothing to worry about, old son,' he said loftily. 'I'll sort things out. I need to think, though. Just keep your trap shut for the mo, won't you?'

Tom's eyes were enormous, but he said nothing.

Alfie thought fast. *A boy aged about twelve wearing a cap* wasn't a good description, but Scotland Yard would send one of their high-up detectives and the high-up detective would have a chat with the police in Bow Street and with the people who had been in the theatre. Sooner or later Alfie's name would come up.

What could he do?

Run!

That was the obvious answer. Get out of London. Lie low! Go missing for a few weeks until the hue and cry died down. His eyes went to the rent box. There was barely enough to pay next week's rent. Would

Jack be able to manage in his absence?

He knew the answer to that. Jack had no authority over Tom. He would allow his younger brother to persuade him to raid the rent box for food and once that happened it would go on. The rent collector would arrive. Would give them seven days' notice. Would call day after day, every day, but there would be no money to pay him. Soon the three remaining boys would all be on the streets and would probably die on one of those nights of frozen fog. Plenty did. The first job the street cleaners had to do in the morning was to get rid of the bodies – dead children, dead dogs, dead old tramps – women and men – dead bodies of the newly homeless. London was no place for those who could not care for themselves.

He couldn't run away. He had to be there to look after them all, to ensure the rent was reserved, that he, his brother and his cousins were fed.

And there was another thing, also. If he left London, this murder might never be solved. Alfie thought highly of his own brains and did not think that most policemen could equal them. He needed to stay around to find the true villain and clear his name. He couldn't trust anyone else.

'I need a disguise,' he said after a minute.

'Dress up as a woman,' sniggered Tom with a look at Alfie's rough hair and grimy face. 'You'd look good, but where would you get the clothes?'

'Wait,' said Alfie slowly. 'Let me think.' Questions were crowding into his head. *Why had the riot been arranged? Was it really a protest about the rise in seat prices, or was it perhaps a way of making sure that no one was looking at the stage while the poison was added to the drink? And who was that small fat man who had given him the free tickets?*

'Tom,' said Alfie. 'I think I know what to do. I'm going to look for a job at Covent Garden Theatre.'

Tom's mouth fell open. 'Covent Garden Theatre! But won't they nab you there?'

'I'm going to dress up as a clown,' said Alfie firmly. 'No one will recognise me then.'

'A clown? You?'

Alfie glared at his cousin. 'What's so funny about that? The geezer that gave me the tickets, he told me that my juggling was good enough.'

Was it possible that the man who gave him the tickets was connected with the murder? 'They're going to have a show with clowns tonight after the opera has finished,' the man had said. 'You should go and watch it. Here are some tickets for you.' He had lots of tickets, Alfie had noticed, as he watched the man's yellow gloves fumble in the pocket.

'The police will get you if you go out,' said Tom.

'I told you that I'll be disguised,' said Alfie impatiently. 'I'll be disguised as a clown.'

'How will you do that?'

'Betty from Monmouth Street,' said Alfie. 'You know her grandma is the old clothes woman? Betty told me that she'd help me if I was ever in trouble – just like I helped her. I'll stay here and you go and get her. Tell her I want to be disguised as a clown. Go on, Tom, get her; go quickly.'

After he had gone, Alfie sat down on the cushion by the fireplace and put his head in his hands. He needed to do some hard thinking.

Why had the man who gave him the tickets wanted to start a riot? What was in it for him? And why was Harry Booth killed?

Alfie tried again to think what the man looked like. Heavy cloak, gloves, a top hat pulled down over his face.

Struggle as he might, Alfie could not remember the face. All the time the man was talking Alfie had continued with his tricks, continued his jokes, hoping desperately that some of the passers-by, hurrying home out of the fog and heavy drizzle, would drop a penny into his cap.

So he had not looked.

He remembered the voice, though. A funny, high-pitched voice.

Perhaps this man had a grudge against the theatre manager; perhaps he was facing the sack.

But why kill Harry Booth? He wasn't important. He just played lots of small parts, like a waiter, or a soldier or a man with a message, or so he had told Alfie the time that he and Jack had helped him to move scenery.

However it happened, Alfie knew one thing: the police needed to arrest someone fast. The person who dared to commit murder in front of Queen Victoria must be brought to justice – and hanged.

And Alfie was their chief suspect.

CHAPTER 4

A TERRIBLE RISK

'You're mad, Alfie!' Betty was a plump, short, curly-haired girl, aged about seventeen. She edged nervously back towards the cellar door. 'You don't want to get mixed up with murder. I've had a night in the cells myself, and I can tell you that it was the longest night of my life.'

'He has to be disguised or they'll pick him up the first time he shows his nose outside the door.' Tom sounded nervous and unsure.

'I'll dress you up as a girl,' said Betty. 'I've got some stuff here in my bag. What's the point of dressing as a clown? That'll make everyone look at you straight away. You'll stand out like a sore thumb on the streets, that you will.'

'I might on the streets,' said Alfie with a grin. 'But I aim to go into Covent Garden Theatre. Once I join the queue there at four o'clock, I'll just be one of a hundred clowns. I won't stir outside the door until then.'

'Covent Garden Theatre!' Betty looked at Tom and then back at Alfie.

'He's mad,' said Tom.

'Worse than mad,' said Betty. 'Everyone's talking about the murder. That place will be crawling with policemen.'

'They won't be looking for me there,' said Alfie with conviction. 'I won't be a boy; I'll be a small man. And I won't sound like a boy. I've been practising a voice while I was waiting for you. It's the voice of Joseph Bishop, you know, the old codger that digs up the bodies from the burying ground.'

He cleared his throat, swallowed hard, and took deep breath. 'Good day to you, my masters,' he said in the hoarse, rusty tones of the grave robber.

'That's good,' said Tom admiringly, but Betty just shuddered.

'Don't do it, Alfie,' she wailed. 'You're mad.'

'I have to.' Alfie was resolute. It was no good arguing with either Betty or Tom, but he knew that he could never get back to his normal life again until this murder was solved. Suddenly he realised that he had forgotten about hunger. Life and liberty were more important. The secret of the murder of Harry Booth would lie in Covent Garden Theatre and somehow or other he had to get in there and ask some questions.

'Come on, Betty,' he said. 'Get that rouge and face paint out! Make sure that you do a good job.'

There were no looking glasses in the cellar, just a dirt-smeared window, so he would have to rely on Betty. Already she had taken scissors, needles and cotton thread from her bag. She had been stitching for her bad-tempered old grandmother since she was a child of five.

'How are you going to get out of here?' asked Tom anxiously.

'It'll be dark by four and the theatre only opens around then,' said Alfie carelessly. 'Tom, old chap, see if you can get us something to eat – beg, borrow or steal, as they say,' he said cheerfully. 'And bring Sammy and Mutsy with you when you come back.'

It would not be much good for Sammy to stay out

too long in that freezing fog – he would lose his voice. As for Tom, at the moment Alfie did not care whether he begged, borrowed or stole as long as he was careful. They all needed food and now Alfie needed to concentrate. The important thing was to think hard about the Covent Garden murder!

But before Tom could move there was the sound of heavy footsteps and then a thunderous knock on the door. And then a shout: 'Open in the name of the law!'

Alfie's eyes darted here and there. He knew now the feelings of a rat that had been driven into a corner. The cellar was no place to hide in. The police knew he lived there. They would not leave before they had searched every inch of it. Sweat broke out on his forehead and he clenched and unclenched his hands. The window! Would it be possible to climb out of it and to bury himself in all of the filth that accumulated in the small sunken area in front of it? He didn't know if the window opened or not. He couldn't ever remember anyone bothering to open it. The smell would have been too bad.

And then as his mind scurried around like an animal in a trap, a miracle occurred! A shout of 'Stop, thief!' A woman's voice screaming! Then the sound of a whistle blowing and heavy footsteps pounding back up the steps to the pavement! Whoever the woman was, Alfie silently blessed her.

'I've got to go,' he said rapidly. Where would he be safe? His mind scanned frantically through various places and rejected them all. He and Betty needed somewhere private; somewhere Alfie could lurk until the light began to fade.

Alfie dashed to the cupboard, took out his father's old cloak, rotten with damp and eaten into holes by moths, and slung it around his shoulders. It trailed on the ground, but not too badly. His father had been a small man. He stood on his toes and groped around at the back of the shelf. First he thought that it had been thrown out, or sold long ago, but then his fingers touched a slimy, mildewed surface. He pulled. It was an old bowler hat – once it had been black, but now it was a poisonous, mouldy green, bashed and with a gaping hole on one side. Alfie snatched it out, clapped it on his head. It came right down over his forehead and rested on his ears. He went to the door and jerked his head to Betty to tell her to follow himself and Tom.

'Meet you at the burying ground in Crown Court,' he said rapidly and ignored her dismayed face. No one wanted to go near that ancient burying ground where dead body was piled on dead body, where bones lay scattered on the surface and the ground oozed with a nameless substance.

But this was good; they would have it to themselves. Joseph Bishop, the grave robber, worked by night and everyone else avoided the place unless they had a body to bury.

'Quick,' he said to her. 'Grab your bag. You go first. Stand on the pavement and look up and down. Just nod if it's all clear. Then I'll slip out and you can follow me after a few minutes. Make sure that no one sees you go.'

'Alfie, I'd be scared to go down that passageway on my own,' whimpered Betty.

Alfie cast a desperate glance up at the street. It was empty. Now was the moment; he could not afford to waste time.

'I'll wait for you just around the corner,' he said impatiently. 'Just count up to sixty and if there's no sign of the police coming, just follow me.'

Could she count up to sixty, he wondered as he edged his way along the soot-blackened buildings and disappeared around the corner of the passageway leading to the burial ground. Twenty would be her limit, he thought.

Alfie had got as far as forty in his mind when he

heard the voice of authority. It was the constable's voice and he was shouting at Betty. 'You just wait a minute, my girl!'

Alfie held his breath; Betty wasn't too bright, and she was terrified of the police. What would she say? Would she betray him?

'Hey, you!' shouted the constable. 'Where's that other boy, the oldest of you? What's his name? Alfie?'

'He's not here. He's gone away.' It was Tom's voice. Alfie didn't know whether that was good or not. Still, Tom would be a better liar than Betty, he supposed.

'*Not – here – he – has – gone – away.*'

Alfie drew a cautious breath of relief. The constable sounded as though he were writing down the answer. That was a relief. He didn't seem to be interested in hunting his prey. Quite possibly the Bow Street Police resented being given orders by the Scotland Yard crowd.

'Where's he gone?' He didn't sound too interested, but once again Alfie held his breath. What would Tom say?

'He's gone to visit his grandmother,' said Betty's voice and Alfie smiled. It sounded good, he thought. Betty's mind was always on her own unpleasant grandmother who made a slave out of her and beat her whenever she was in a bad mood. *Grandmother* was obviously the first word that came into her head.

'*Gone – to – visit – his – grandmother.*'

Alfie quivered with impatience. He could just imagine the policeman's pencil laboriously tracing the words into his notebook.

'Well, I'd better be off back to the station; keep out of trouble, you two.'

Alfie smiled. It sounded like PC 23, not a bad fellow. He hoped that Betty would wait until he was out of sight before she turned into Broad Court.

They should be alone there. Only a truly desperate person would choose to come down this grim passageway to the burying ground.

CHAPTER 5

HIDE!

'Come on,' said Alfie impatiently when Betty eventually appeared. He kept well back from the Bow Street entrance, but by listening hard he guessed that there were not many people passing by. The fog was bad and there were very few shops in that section of the street; the few people who had been around had not returned since the chase after the thief. Now was the time for him to vanish.

The passageway to the burying ground was dark, hemmed in on either side by tall, windowless walls. It was very narrow and on a damp, foggy day it smelt of evil, nameless things. Alfie and Betty walked silently side by side. The stench would get worse as they went along and Alfie knew that by the time they reached the burying ground it would become almost unbearable.

Even so, it was the only place that he could think of where the police would not choose to go; where the search would not be worth the unpleasantness. It was the only place where a boy who was wanted for murder could be safe for a few hours before darkness fell.

Betty clutched his arm suddenly and he did not push her away. It was good of her to come so quickly, and good of her to risk trouble with the police by helping Alfie put on a disguise. And it was extra good of her to brave the terrors of the Drury Lane burying ground.

But there was a sound of footsteps. Two sets of footsteps tramping up the alleyway. Alfie groaned to himself. Was nothing going right for him today? He knew what was happening. The lamplighter was coming up from Drury Lane to light the gas lamp outside the burying ground.

And – what was worse – he would have a policeman with him. No lamplighter would brave that place without a police escort. Alfie could hear their voices now.

'Come on, quick,' he said to Betty as he turned back towards Bow Street. He would just have to risk it. Better to meet a policeman in a crowded street than an empty alleyway.

However, there was no sign of the constable when they came out. Where could they go? Suddenly Alfie had an idea.

'Follow me,' he whispered to Betty as he crossed the street and dived down another alleyway, then another and then another, pausing at each entrance only long enough to make sure that Betty was following him.

Now they were out in front of the church of St Paul's, the church near Covent Garden Theatre. There was a Punch and Judy show going on under the marble arches in front of the building and a few people were watching it. Alfie slid along the side until he came to the belfry at the back. The bell was tolling – must be someone dead in the parish, thought Alfie, counting the numbers – someone old. Would it ever stop? Betty was shivering with cold and with fright. Sixty-five, thought Alfie and then abruptly the bell stopped and the bell-ringer came out, slamming the door behind him.

Once the man's footsteps died away, Alfie stole

forward silently. He turned the handle cautiously. No, the door was not locked. He grabbed Betty's hand and pulled her inside. A dim light came through the window from the gas lamp outside.

'Oh, Alfie,' whimpered Betty. 'I'm scared of this place. They say it's haunted. They say that the devil didn't want the church to have a bell. Once he burnt the place down with the fires from hell.'

'Come on,' whispered Alfie impatiently. 'What did you bring me? Be quick and then you can go.' She would forget about ghosts once she got the clothes out, he thought. Betty was clothes-mad.

Betty had done her best. She had brought with her a much-darned silk waistcoat and a much-worn shirt with frilly sleeves. Both had been badly torn, but sewn together with several neat patches. She handed them to him from her basket and then produced a pair of men's long baggy pin-striped trousers. Alfie stared at them in dismay.

'They're too big,' giggled Betty. She held them up. 'Put them on over your own trousers,' she advised and Alfie pulled them on while Betty held the shirt and waistcoat. They reached down well below his own trousers and trailed on the ground. He rolled them up.

'Don't do that,' said Betty. 'Leave them down.

Now perhaps they won't notice that you have no shoes. I'm sure that clowns shouldn't have bare feet.'

The shirt was better. It was made from silk, he thought, and had fancy cuffs at the ends of the sleeves. They reminded him of the hand that had come from behind the curtain and dropped the poison into the glass of port. What was the odd thing about that hand? He shut his eyes and tried to visualize it.

'Be careful with that shirt,' warned Betty. 'I've put hours of work into it.'

Alfie pulled it over his head. It was extremely large. Although he had left his jacket on underneath, it drooped in folds down to his waist. The sight seemed to send Betty into a fit of laughing.

'Shut up,' hissed Alfie. 'Don't make such a noise. You might rouse that devil.'

'Alfie!' wailed Betty, clutching his arm.

'Only joking,' said Alfie hastily. 'Do my face now. You got any of that white stuff? I'd like to be one of them scary clowns – I've seen one once – big white face and black all around his eyes.'

'You'll have to make do with this.' Betty showed him a small pot. 'Got it from a gentleman friend of mine,' she said proudly. 'Ever such nice stuff. Shame to waste it on . . . oh my God, what was that?'

'Just a bit of mist,' said Alfie quickly. He himself didn't like the way a strange clump of white mist seemed to be oozing through the opening high above their heads, but he did his best to make his voice sound casual. He didn't want Betty running off before she finished the job of turning him into a clown.

'I should have washed your face first,' said Betty as she applied the creamy stuff to his dirty skin. 'It's all turning grey.'

'That's good,' said Alfie. 'That stuff looks too biscuity-coloured. Grey will look better. Now do my eyes. What have you got for them?'

'Got a pot of lampblack, here,' said Betty. 'I just rub a bit on my eyelids, but you can have as much as you like. That's free. Grandmother's eyes are getting bad and she is always fussing me about cleaning the soot off the inside of the lamp.'

'Make big circles around my eyes,' ordered Alfie. 'Giant-sized ones! Make me look like the devil . . .' He tried to remember what the clergyman had said about the devil when he had gone to church with Sammy once. Something about him roaming the earth with a mouth like fire and eyes like smouldering coals – that would be the right look, he thought with satisfaction. 'Make me a huge red mouth,' he said, baring his teeth.

'There,' said Betty after a few minutes. 'That's the best I can do. I'm sorry, Alfie, I must go. You know what Grandmother is like. When Tom come I told her that he had a message to say that a place on Bloomsbury Street had thrown out some old clothes. She'll be expecting me back any minute. I'll have to tell her that it was all old rags.'

She didn't wait for his answer but seized her basket and slipped out of the door.

After she had gone Alfie took up his father's old cloak from the ground and put it around his shoulders. Then he put on the bowler hat. In spite of the hole, it would keep his head warm.

But his bare feet were freezing. He crouched down upon the stone floor, tucked his feet under him, wrapped his two arms around him, hunched his shoulders, sank his chin down upon his chest – and shivered. And then, extraordinarily, he must have fallen asleep. He woke with a start. The bells of St Martin-in-the-Fields chimed the call to vespers.

Alfie jumped to his feet. He had little interest in churches, but one thing every Londoner knew was that once one bell started then every bell in the neighbourhood followed. He had better get out of here, he thought, and grabbed the door handle.

But he was too late.

Heavy footsteps were tramping down the path. Voices raised.

'No, constable, haven't seen no boy around here. Ask the Punch and Judy folk. They're just packing up now.'

And then the door was pulled open.

CHAPTER 6

WHERE IS YOUR BROTHER?

Sammy knew that someone was looking at him. Nobody, not even Alfie, knew how Sammy could do this. He had been blind from the time that he was a tiny child, completely and absolutely blind, but somehow the sense that had been taken away from him had left him with his other senses sharpened to an almost supernatural degree. His sense of smell was extraordinary. His hearing was pin-sharp. He knew every step, every cough – and could identify most of the people around by some combination of hearing and smell.

And, perhaps by some sixth sense, Sammy, like a

dog, could tell whether someone meant harm, or meant good.

And this person, he reckoned, meant harm.

Who was it? A man, guessed Sammy. Somehow the restless movement seemed more like a man than a woman. He could hear something now, perhaps it was the creak of leather boots, and then the rubbing together of leather gloves, the faint whiff of cigar smoke – yes, decided Sammy, it definitely was a man.

But what did he want? He was standing nearby – not too close. The song had ended. The man had not put anything in the cloth cap on the ground. Even if Sammy had missed the fall of a coin into the empty cap, Mutsy would have wagged his tail – he always wagged a polite thank you when anyone gave coins – and that would have been impossible to miss. Mutsy had a very long tail and it was fringed with tangled plumes of long hair. When Mutsy wagged his tail, it was like a storm wind rising and fanning everyone in the near vicinity.

Why was the man interested in him? A blind boy singing? Was it the song? Sammy sang it again, hopefully. Perhaps now a coin would fall.

But nothing happened.

Sammy could not understand. He had begun to feel a little uneasy.

And then he heard the man take a few steps towards him.

For a moment nothing was said – none of the usual, 'You have a beautiful voice, what's the name of that song?' or, occasionally, some charitable person, 'Aren't you cold singing out here in this weather?'

This man said nothing. What did he want?

And then he spoke, a strange voice. 'Is that your dog?' was what the man said.

Sammy felt relieved. So the man was just admiring Mutsy.

'Yes, it is,' he said.

'Clever dog.' The man had come nearer now. The smell of fine cloth, good leather and of expensive cigars was more distinct. This was a toff; Sammy was sure of that.

But he didn't speak like a toff. He spoke like a cockney – like a cockney, but with a strange high-pitched voice. He puzzled Sammy.

'Can do a bit of juggling, that dog, isn't that right?'

'That's right,' replied Sammy. He wished that Alfie were here. Alfie would have enjoyed this. The man was no more a cockney than Queen Victoria herself. A cockney would have said: *ain't that so*, not *isn't that right?*

'I've seen him with another boy. Your brother was it?'

And now, suddenly, Sammy knew who the man was. What had Alfie said: *Funny voice – a bit squeaky, like*. This was the mysterious stranger who had given Alfie the tickets.

But why did he want Alfie? Was it just to give him the promised shilling? Or was there some other reason?

Why had this man arranged a riot to happen minutes before Harry Booth was murdered?

'You might as well go home. I'll go with you. I want to see your brother.' The squeaky-voiced stranger broke through Sammy's thoughts. 'No harm,' the voice continued. 'No harm to him, none at all. Just want to have a word with him.'

And it was that expression, *no harm* that made Sammy's mind up. Why say that?

'Just going, sir,' he said. He fumbled on the ground, felt Mutsy's cold nose guiding his hand, picked up the cap, held it in front of his face and behind its cover, put his mouth close to Mutsy's hairy ear and said in a whisper quieter than a sigh, 'Smithfield, Mutsy', then he straightened up and took a firm grasp of the knotted rope around Mutsy's neck.

'Don't you have to give him some order?' Did the man sound curious – or perhaps slightly uneasy, tense, maybe?

Sammy laughed in a natural way. 'Mutsy knows what to do,' he said.

'I'll follow you, then,' said the high-pitched voice.

'Yes, sir,' said Sammy. Smithfield market with its hundreds of people, hundreds of stalls, hundreds of animals would be a good place to get lost.

Sammy certainly was not going to lead this man to the cellar in Bow Street.

Alfie had been seen on the stage; this man might be planning to hand him over to the police. Or worse.

Sammy did some hard thinking. Could this man have anything to do with the murder on the theatre stage?

Could he, perhaps, be the murderer?

Sammy had once met a murderer and he knew one thing.

A man who has murdered once will murder again.

CHAPTER 7

ON
THE RUN

Alfie knew there was no way that he could escape. Even if he could get past the bell-ringer, there was still the policeman outside – not far away. He shrank into the corner and turned his face towards the wall.

And then a beam of light lit up the wall ahead of him. It was no good. He had been seen. He turned around slowly. The man had a bull's eye lantern in his hand and he was shining it directly at Alfie.

But the man did not call out. Why not?

In a second, Betty's story about the devil flashed through Alfie's mind. He bared his teeth, picturing the effect of his huge red mouth and the black-circled

41

eyes. He did not move, just stayed very still. The man backed away, and then turned and fled. Alfie was tempted to follow him, but didn't. Surely the fellow would come to his senses if he saw Alfie run.

Instead he reached out, seized the bell rope and slowly clanged out the hour – four strokes – that was what the bell from St Martin's had pealed.

When the echo from the last bell died away, Alfie peered out. There was no sign of the man. The devil ringing the church bell had just finished him off, thought Alfie with a grin. He slipped along beside the wall.

'I saw him, your reverence! I saw him as plain as I see you. And he rang the bell! I didn't ring the bell! The devil himself did that!' The man's voice was trembling. Alfie grinned to himself as he crept silently along in the shadow of the wall.

'Have you been drinking, man?'

Alfie crammed a knuckle into his mouth to stop himself giggling. He saw the queue of clowns as soon as he rounded the corner. It was even bigger than last night's. The news of the murder had not put anyone off. On the contrary, it had brought fifty or sixty others, all dressed as clowns and all eager to have a part in this notorious theatre. Alfie joined them. He looked nervously at the costumes and the face paint. Everything looked so much more professional than his. Even to himself, when he looked down, he thought that he looked pretty shabby.

There were no policemen around, luckily. It was getting dark and in the vegetable market the stallholders were placing their unsold wares into carts, barrows and baskets. Alfie kept his father's bowler hat pulled well down over his face; he had glimpsed an old enemy, a woman called Mary Robinson, and he had no wish to encounter her.

A lot of the clowns were quite elderly, he thought. They would not be as good as Alfie when it came to turning somersaults and juggling. On the other hand, they might be better at telling jokes.

Still, he had many times managed to hold an audience at a street corner on wet and foggy days, so surely he would be as good as these old fellows.

That's if he got a chance to perform. The queue seemed to move very slowly.

He was beginning to get worried when the church bells chimed for the half hour. Would he even get a chance to prove how good he was?

'Always had his nose in other people's business; that was Harry Booth for you.'

Two clowns, dressed alike except that one had green spangles and a blue wig, and one red spangles and an orange wig, were ahead of him in the queue. They had been chattering about various theatres – Drury Lane, The Royal at Haymarket and the Lyceum on the Strand. They seemed to know a lot about these places, but Alfie had lost interest and had stopped listening until he heard the last words.

'That was Harry,' agreed the clown with green spangles.

Alfie held his breath and willed them to go on. What was it that Sammy had said? *Might have been a blackmailer, mightn't he?*

'Reckon that's what done for him,' the first clown said gloomily. 'Pushed someone a bit too far, that's what he did – he would always want the extra few shillings. You mark my words, Lucky.'

'You're right, Joey,' agreed Lucky. After a minute's silence he said with an air of surprise. 'What would you say to that Francis Fairburn – they say that he was furious with Harry Booth on account of the fact that he stole his girl, Rosa . . . he's working here and all.'

Alfie feared that would be the end of the conversation – but Joey was still chewing over the sensational murder.

'More likely that other business with that actor that done for him – you know that baby-faced cove – the fellow that used to act all the smart-young-man-about-town parts? What was his name, Lucky?'

Some other clowns ahead in the queue turned around and listened with interest. They all seemed very friendly with each other – knew each other's names and shared each other's memories. The chatter in the queue was mostly along the lines of 'Do you remember . . .' or 'What's he doing now?'

Lots of them were in pairs and each member of the pair was dressed similarly to the other, noticed Alfie, feeling rather depressed about his own outfit. One clown had short bright blue trousers, reaching just between the knee and ankle, a violently red blazer and a yellow shirt with an enormous bow tie and his friend was the same except his trousers were red and his blazer blue. Most had frilly sleeves peeping from under their jackets and all had fuzzy wigs and strange hats. It was a strange sight to see all of those blank white faces, red mouths and circled eyes listening so intently to the conversation about Harry Booth.

'You talking about John Osborne?' enquired Lucky.

'That's the one. You remember what happened.

Harry Booth was supposed to come on stage and pretend to slash his face with a knife. Usual business. Harry slashes, John Osborne screams, John Osborne claps a handkerchief full of red stuff to his face, takes it away, drips blood, faints, young lady faints . . .'

'All the usual routine,' agreed a man in front.

'Ah, but it wasn't, you see,' retorted Joey, who seemed to have become quite jolly with the audience that he had listening to his story. Even more clowns, from further up the queue, had now turned around and were listening intently. Joey looked from face to face and then hissed dramatically.

'It wasn't the same old routine at all, because the blood was real, the cuts on the face were real and the knife was not a wooden knife, painted grey. It was a real knife and it had an edge on it as sharp as a razor.'

'Harry Booth denied it, of course.' Lucky decided to lend a hand.

'Of course he did,' said Joey. 'Wouldn't you? Swore that he didn't know that the knife had been changed. He got someone to say that he hadn't been near the stage after the props were put out, so it all stayed a mystery. The fact remained that John Osborne never got another chance to play the smart-young-man-about-town parts. A few of them went to Harry

Booth, so I suppose he got some luck from the . . .' He paused and then said in that strange high-pitched voice that all the clowns used, '. . . from the unfortunate mistake.' And then he did a little dance and slapped hands with Lucky.

Everyone laughed heartily. Alfie began to think that Joey, despite his long face and his lugubrious manner, might be one to get a job. He was quite a comic.

What about himself? Did he have a chance? He looked down at his costume and blushed – perhaps it might have been better to have put the waistcoat under the jacket – but the waistcoat was made for an enormously fat man. It would just look silly. At least the jacket bulked it out a bit. He gazed dubiously down at the long baggy trousers and his bare feet. The other clowns did have ridiculous trousers, but they weren't barefoot; they had enormous shoes tied with enormous laces. Perhaps he should give up the idea, he thought, pulling the over-sized cloak more tightly around him. Perhaps he should just slink away; lie low for a while.

And then Lucky spoke again. 'What happened to John Osborne, Joey?' he asked.

'Got a job here.' Joey jerked his head at the theatre.

'Stagehand.' He looked around expectantly and Lucky obliged him. His voice was low and dramatic when he stated to his eager audience, 'So John Osborne was here last night when Harry Booth fell dead on the stage.'

CHAPTER 8

A THEATRE FULL OF CLOWNS

Alfie stood behind the curtain and peered through. He was standing in exactly the same place as the murderer had stood the night before, he thought. A policeman was poking around in the background, but Alfie ignored him. He had been a bit nervous in the beginning but then he realised that the man, by now, was sick of clowns and was quite uninterested in any of them.

Joey and Lucky were in the middle of their act. Eight clowns had already been chosen and only two more places remained. Alfie felt worried. He hadn't realised that clowns needed to be in groups. At least, all of the previous acts had been clowns in twos or threes.

Joey and Lucky were not doing too well. It wasn't much of an audience – just one man sitting out in the front stalls of the theatre – and that one man didn't laugh, clap, or cheer. He just sat there and stared, in a bored way, at the stage. Alfie looked across the stage at him. He almost felt like going home. If the manager looked so bored by these two experienced clowns, then there would be no hope for him.

And then suddenly an idea came to him. He thought about it for a second and then decided to do it. Already the manager had turned to take up the white handkerchief that was the signal for the act to stop and the next set of clowns to come on stage. Joey and Lucky were not going to get the job. He might as well try.

And he would wear his cloak and his bowler hat. He didn't have the tall, pointed hat that the other clowns wore and now that he looked at his outfit – the man's waistcoat with the blackened, tattered jacket showing though it, the man's baggy trousers sliding down over his hips and displaying his own ragged trousers – well, the whole outfit was useless.

Unless he was something different . . .

He would be a tramp! A clown-tramp!

Rapidly Alfie ran on to the stage.

'Good evening, my masters,' he said in Joseph Bishop's rough, hoarse voice.

Joey and Lucky both gave him furious glances, but he ignored them. As they carried on with their routine, he danced around behind them, copying everything they did, echoing everything they said, deliberately hitching at the too-big trousers, clutching at his bowler hat and falling over the too-long cloak. When they began to juggle, he kept throwing himself at the balls in the air. If he missed, he stuck his finger through the hole in his bowler hat and mimed despair, grimacing violently at the bars of the metal gantry overhead.

When Joey threw a custard pie at Lucky, Alfie launched himself between the two men, caught it and immediately began to eat it. The pastry was rock hard and the custard lumpy, but to Alfie, who had not eaten for almost two days, it tasted fantastic. He was determined to finish it before he got thrown out. Joey gave an indignant shout and charged across the stage towards him, but Alfie took off his bowler hat and slung it hard. It hit Joey in the middle and he dropped to the ground, groaning loudly. Just fooling, thought Alfie as he hastily gobbled down the last mouthful. Joey had decided to go along with the new man in their act.

And at that moment came a laugh from the

manager and a shout of, 'You'll do! We'll take all three of you for tonight.'

And then he got to his feet and shouted, 'David, tell the rest to go away. We've got enough now.'

'Who do you think you are? Muscling in like that?' Lucky rounded furiously on Alfie as soon as they were backstage.

'Sorry about that,' said Alfie, licking the remains of the custard from his fingers. Joey was the leader so he addressed himself to him. 'I thought I'd have no chance unless I cottoned on to a flash act like yours.'

'That's all right,' said Joey in a stately way after a few seconds where he seemed to be turning over matters in his mind. After all, thought Alfie, watching him hopefully, they had got the job and most of the others had been turned away.

'That was a good idea, the custard pie one,' said Lucky, cheerful again. 'Never saw no one eat one of them things before. It'll stick in your stomach like a bar of lead. Still, you're young!'

'Tasted good to me,' said Alfie. If only they had another pie he would have eaten that too.

'He's a sour old so-and-so that manager, ain't he?' Lucky had turned away from Alfie and addressed himself to Joey.

'Not surprising.' Joey gave a quick look around but all the rest of the clowns had gone from behind the stage – even the policeman had moved away and was now prowling the gallery, peering under seats in the vain hope of discovering a reason for the murder.

'Not surprising,' he repeated. 'They say that the theatre is going to go broke. If this rioting goes on for many more nights and audience numbers keep dropping off, then he'll be bankrupt and that will be the end of him and of all his fine ideas. He'll be locked up in a debtors' prison.'

'There are too many of them theatres, these days,' said Lucky, shaking his head in a gloomy way. 'Stands to reason they can't all make money. Look at Drury Lane Theatre – only a stone's throw from Covent Garden. One or other of them should shut down and then the other could make a decent living. I heard they're in a bit of trouble too – that bloke at Drury Lane, that manager – he's in bad trouble – that's what I heard anyways.'

And then with a nod at him they both went off, leaving Alfie to sit on a box backstage and wait for the evening show.

Things were looking better for him. The custard and rock-hard pastry had filled his stomach and the theatre was packed with clowns. No one would notice him.

Even so, he wished that he were back in the cellar with his gang and his faithful Mutsy.

But this murder would have to be solved and Alfie had to put all of his brains to work. He now had the names of two people who might have murdered Harry Booth. There was Francis Fairburn, who was in love with this Rosa, but she preferred Harry Booth – and then there was the other fellow, John Osborne. That was more serious. Harry Booth had slashed his face with a knife and destroyed his good looks.

Or could the murder have anything to do with the sour-faced manager, who was worried about money? Could Harry Booth have had some responsibility for the riots that threatened to shut down the theatre? Was Harry Booth trying to make sure that no more seats were sold for Covent Garden Theatre? If that happened the manager would go bust!

Was going bankrupt and having to be locked up in a debtors' prison enough reason to commit murder?

Alfie thought it was.

Prison was a dreadful thing. And that's where he would be heading if the true murderer wasn't found soon!

CHAPTER 9

SAMMY
IS PURSUED

When Sammy walked through London with his brother, Alfie always described the route and they often played a game where Sammy guessed the name of the street and Alfie told him if he was right. A correct guess meant that Sammy got a point, and a wrong guess meant that Alfie got a point. So Alfie tried to lead him into all sorts of strange places and Sammy got better and better at guessing.

Temple Bar was one of the easy places. That was at the top of the Strand and Sammy always recognised it because he could hear how the horse-drawn carriages and hansom cabs all slowed down here.

Mutsy was taking him past Temple Bar now, and they were passing the Temple Inns. Even on this foggy day Sammy could feel the wind from the River Thames on his right – not so much a wind, perhaps, as an increase in the cold damp striking against his cheek wherever there was a gap in the buildings.

The man still followed. From time to time, he dropped back – Mutsy walked fast and Sammy, holding securely to the knotted rope around the big dog's neck, kept to his pace.

Now they were turning. Going uphill; their backs were to the river. And that was good. The air from the river was behind them – not much of an air movement, not even a breeze. But it was enough for Sammy. The smell of leather, wool and cigars drifted up to him.

The man was still behind, still following.

Smithfield market was crowded as usual. The thunder of cartwheels, the neighing of horses, the squealing of pigs, the frantic bellowing of cattle, the cackle of geese, the crowing of cocks, the shouts, yells and continuous cries of 'Come, buy! Come, buy!' filled the air.

Smells, too! Smithfield was full of them. Thousands of animals dropped filth on the ground: there was an appalling stench from everything. There was no way that Sammy could either hear or smell the stranger with the squeaky voice. He would just have to hope that the man would be too repulsed by the place and would go away, or decide to try again on another day.

The problem was Mutsy.

Poor Mutsy – he was clever, but not as clever as his young master. Sammy grimaced. There was no way that he could make Mutsy understand that he wanted to lose himself among the great swathe of beasts. Mutsy was very protective of Sammy and carefully made sure that he kept him away from danger.

So he took Sammy away from the noise and confusion of the animal market and towards the stalls around the west side of Smithfield where no cattle, pigs or sheep were allowed. Sammy had to go along helplessly, not daring to let go of the knotted rope around Mutsy's neck.

And then an arm seized his. A voice spoke in his ear. 'I'm afraid that you are lost, young man! I don't believe that you live anywhere near here at all. You are playing games with me, aren't you? Come with me and I'll get you out of here.'

The stranger had Sammy in his power!

Was there any way that he could get free of him?

Sammy didn't know what to do. How could he

make Mutsy understand that he didn't want this man? Mutsy was used to charitable strangers taking into their heads that Sammy needed to be led across the road. Mutsy would obey any order from Alfie or Sammy. Sammy just had to say, 'Seize him, Mutsy,' and the dog would grab the man and hold him until ordered to let him go, but it was too dangerous.

The problem was that no one would listen to a poor boy. If a toff – and Sammy was sure that this man was a toff – spoke to a policeman in a posh accent and told him that Mutsy was dangerous, then the dog would probably be shot. He dared not risk it so he walked on silently, the dog on one side and the man on the other, allowing himself to be led. He would give it a few minutes, he thought, and after that he would twist suddenly, break free and start to run, relying on Mutsy to bring him safely through the crowds.

But then he suddenly became aware of something. Mutsy was on his right-hand side and the man on his left. This meant that it was the man's right hand that held Sammy's arm.

And there was something strange about that hand.

CHAPTER 10

SARAH LENDS A HAND

'Are you telling me that Alfie has gone down to the theatre?' Sarah gazed incredulously at Tom and Jack.

'I wasn't here,' explained Jack. 'Tom told me. Alfie got himself dressed up by Betty and his face painted and all that and then off he went.'

'With that old cloak around him,' supplemented Tom. 'Sarah, you haven't anything for me to eat, have you?'

'No,' said Sarah shortly. She didn't get too much to eat herself. Today the food had been poor – burnt potatoes and a bit of watery gravy was all that was given to the scullery maid.

'Well, I haven't been able to get anything,' complained Tom. 'There was nothing that I could nick and everyone is just trying to get in out of the fog. I tried begging, but I didn't get a halfpenny. I couldn't even borrow the crossing boy's broom. He was hungry too. I'm fed up with this. I feel like going off and joining Maggie the Plucker's pickpocket gang. At least she feeds them.'

'And most of them end up in prison,' said Jack. 'And then she gets some new boys. She don't care.' He sounded irritable. Jack did not often argue with Tom.

'Where's Sammy?' Sarah looked around the little cellar with concern. Sammy was usually comfortably tucked into the corner by the fire, but there was no sign of him.

'Don't know!' Tom gave a shrug and then when Jack looked at him, he said reluctantly, 'I had a look around but I couldn't see him nowhere. I reckoned he had gone home by himself. He had Mutsy with him,' he added hastily as he saw a look of anger on Sarah's face. He addressed himself to his brother. 'Jack, I'm hungry; goodness knows when Alfie will be back. He might kip down in the theatre for that matter. Bet he gets plenty to eat there! Can't we take some money out of the rent box? We'll put it back tomorrow.'

'Don't you dare,' said Sarah firmly. 'You know that Alfie says that must never be touched. Don't let him do it, Jack. As for you, Tom, you should be ashamed of yourself. You go back out there and find Sammy. It's time he was in, out of the fog. Anyway,' she finished, looking at his furious face, 'the chances are that Sammy has earned some money. You go and find him. Just keep asking if anyone has seen a blind boy singing with a big hairy dog beside him.' There were plenty of blind boys in London, she knew, but Mutsy and Sammy made a fairly memorable pair.

After Tom had sulkily gone out, Sarah sat down and warmed her hands by the fire. She wasn't too worried about Sammy – Sammy had plenty of initiative; if one place didn't work, he would move on to another. Tom was so idle that he hadn't bothered looking around, but made straight for home once he didn't find Sammy immediately.

She was worried about Alfie, though. She, like he, had seen the posters. She, like he, realised the danger – that Alfie would be used as a scapegoat for a murder that happened right under the eyes of the Queen of England, herself.

But Alfie would not allow himself to fear. She knew

his reckless nature. His disguise of a clown, she guessed, would not be very good. Betty was not too bright and she and her grandmother scratched a living by cobbling together some terrible old rags to make clothes that only the very poor would wear. No, sooner or later Alfie would be spotted. Even now he might be on his way to the cells at Bow Street.

How could she help? It wouldn't do any good sitting by the fire sharing gloomy thoughts with Jack, or fighting with Tom, or, worse, going back to the small, dark, damp bedroom behind the scullery in the house where she worked. Inspector Denham had got her this job and he had persuaded the housekeeper to allow Sarah to stop work every day at six o'clock – in order to educate herself at the ragged school. The school was gone now, but Sarah still left every day at six. Often a sinkful of dishes would be there waiting for her when she returned, but it was worth it to escape for a while.

She would go down to Covent Garden Theatre. The performance would not start for another couple of hours. Judging by the state of the place last night they would need plenty of help to get everywhere spick and span by the time it opened.

* * *

It wasn't hard. Sarah came to the back door, said that she was a scullery maid, and after being cross-examined on the name of her employer, their address and how many hours she worked and what sort of cleaning she was permitted to do, was offered sixpence for a couple of hours' work.

'You'd better start backstage,' said a brisk woman. 'The actors make such a fuss if the dressing rooms aren't just so, but today all the regular staff have been too busy cleaning the boxes – you should have seen the mess on some of those beautiful carvings! Or the stalls, you wouldn't believe it. Dreadful, it was! Disgraceful!'

Even more dreadful than murder? thought Sarah, firmly repressing a giggle. However, she silently picked up a broom, a mop and a feather duster and slotted them into a bucket. The woman followed her and watched for a while as she set to work cleaning the starring lady's dressing room in as professional and efficient a way as she could.

After a few minutes the woman gave a nod. 'I can see that you're a good worker,' she said. 'If you want to come around tomorrow night, I can give you a couple of hours' work again.'

'What shall I do when I have finished the dressing rooms?' asked Sarah meekly and was pleased when the woman told her to do the stage itself.

'We've had the usual nonsense about clowns coming and doing their acts. What we want ten new clowns every night for, I couldn't tell you! Anyway, one of the silly fellows let his custard pie slip down on to the floor and there's that to clean up.'

Pity Mutsy isn't here, though Sarah. He would enjoy cleaning a custard pie from the floor. Her mind went to Alfie. But she did not dare go to look for him. First of all those dressing rooms for the stars had to look as shiningly clean as she could make them.

By the time she got to the stage there was no sign of Alfie. He would have hidden himself, of course. Quickly she scrubbed the floor, praying that it would dry before the performance. At least it would be clean and no dust could rise up and spoil the throats of the singers. There were a few clowns sitting on the seats in the pit, talking quietly to each other. She wished that she could listen but the noise of her brisk scrubbing filled her ears and nothing could be heard above that.

And then her heart stopped for a moment.

Two policemen strode on stage, one carrying a small glass phial. The first policeman was saying something over his shoulder to the other. Sarah did not hear that but she paused, dipping her scrubbing brush into the bucket, and the reply was quite clear and distinct.

'If we could just prove that he handled this, then he is as good as hanged!'

'Nah,' exclaimed the other man. 'How could you prove a thing like that? These phials are ten-a-penny. Every chemist shop has a stack of them.'

'Officer!' There was a shout from the back and then a man appeared and walked down the aisle until he stood under the stage. It must be the manager, thought Sarah, looking at him out of the corner of her eye as she wrung out the mop into her bucket. He had an air of authority and was very well dressed, in a shiny frock coat, tight black trousers strapped under his shoes and a snowy-white starched shirt.

'Something interesting here,' he went on, holding out a bundle of tickets. Each was just a half, torn off the night before, thought Sarah remembering Alfie's tickets. 'There's been fraud,' continued the manager. 'Over half of the standing-place tickets given in for the pit and the gallery are not the right ones. Someone has printed fake tickets with our name on them. Come and see for yourselves.'

'Well, that is interesting,' said the first policeman. He seemed cheered at the prospect of something to do.

'Come on,' he said to the second policeman, who was still staring at the glass phial. 'Leave that there.' He looked after the manager who was now striding up the aisle, lowered his voice and said in an undertone that only Sarah could have heard, 'For goodness' sake, stop looking at that thing. You know our orders. Arrest that boy. He'll be convicted as easy as anything. And when he's hanged there'll be one varmint less in London.'

CHAPTER 11

SILENT WITNESS

'Sarah,' said a voice cautiously.

Sarah whirled around. The dustpan slipped from her hand – most of its contents landing on the small table by the wall.

'Alfie, you startled me!' Sarah looked with dismay at the layer of dust now covering the table. Even Alfie's strange appearance with his clown make-up, his jacket plainly visible under the patched waistcoat and worn-out shirt and the baggy trousers drooping down over his skinny hips did not draw a smile from her.

Anxiously and carefully, Sarah edged the dust back into the pan. She didn't want the clean floor to get dirty again. In her job as a scullery maid a mistake like that would earn her a blow from an upper servant. She gave a quick glance around; luckily there was no one watching. She just had to get everything shining again as soon as possible.

'Sarah,' whispered Alfie. 'There are two people working here who might have had a motive to murder Harry Booth – two chaps that hated him. Harry Booth scarred the face of one of them – John Osborne was his name. The other was Francis Fairburn – Harry Booth stole Francis Fairburn's girl and then there's the theatre manager – he's someone that we'll have to investigate as well . . .'

'Wait till I do this and then we can —' Suddenly Sarah stopped.

The dust from the floor of the stage was made up of a mixture of grime and of varnish ground to a pale grey, fine powder by feet: feet striding the stage, feet fidgeting, feet walking, feet dancing and feet running. This fine powder from her dustpan had fallen on the table, but it had also covered the glass phial.

And outlined by the dust were the prints of greasy fingers; a broad thumb on one side and, on the other side, three fingers.

Sarah stared at the glass phial. She opened her

mouth to speak and then turned her head in alarm at the sound of a door opening noisily.

'Shh, they're coming back,' she whispered. 'That's a policeman. Quick, hide – go now.'

Alfie was gone in a flash, sliding between the two halves of the curtain, his bare feet making no sound on the wooden floor. By the time the policeman appeared, she was alone on the stage.

Sarah was trembling. She was pleased to feel her knees shake and hoped that she looked even paler than usual when one of the two policeman came back down the aisle between the seats. Sarah did not try to hide, but waited for him with her head hanging. Now was the moment for her performance on stage. She hoped it would be a convincing one.

'Hey, you girl, have you seen . . .' and then, with a note of relief in his voice, as he spotted the phial, he said, 'There it is!'

Sarah faced him. 'I'm very sorry, sir,' she said, allowing her voice to quiver. 'I had a bit of an accident. I spilt the dirt from the pan. Look at the phial. It's all covered in dust.'

'That's all right, girl,' he said in quite a kind way. 'Don't worry about it. That'll brush off.'

He reached out, but before he could touch it Sarah

gave a gasp. 'Don't touch it, sir; don't touch it. Look! Look, it's got the print of the murderer on it!'

'Murderer!' He said the word slowly. He withdrew his hand and knelt on the ground, ignoring the wet on the board and stared hard at the phial. Then he looked up at her. 'What do you mean?' he asked.

'I'm sorry, sir!' Sarah gulped.

'Officer Grey.' He said the words almost mechanically, still staring at the finger marks on the phial.

'I'm sorry, Officer Grey, I couldn't help hearing what you said a minute ago. I was cleaning.'

'And a good job you've made of it, too.' He got up, looked ruefully at the damp patches on his knees and went across to the edge of the stage. Sarah's eyes followed him. He was fiddling with the gas pipes that ran along the edge. Sarah was glad that she had given them a good dust and polish. They had been black with grime.

Officer Grey took a box of matches from the pocket of his waistcoat, struck one and then bent down. Sarah could hear a soft hiss and then smelt the sickly smell of gas. Officer Grey put the match to the tiny nozzle and a jet of flame leapt up, pointing directly at the candle-shaped block of lime. Almost immediately that began to glow, the white light spreading rapidly until the whole block glowed. After a minute the limelight was strong enough to hurt her eyes. Officer Grey came back to the table and very carefully, placing his thumb at the bottom of the phial and his forefinger over the top opening, grasped the small bottle. He picked it up and carried it over to the limelight.

'You can see them easy now, Officer Grey.' Sarah allowed her voice to get quite eager. She looked carefully at his face. He was frowning slightly. Her heart gave an excited leap.

'Terrible the way fingers leave marks on glasses, isn't it?' she said in a chatty way. 'It's something that I learnt when I first went into service. The parlour maid always gave the glasses an extra polish after I had washed them just in case there was a print left on one of them. She used to say that men were the worst. Their hands were greasier. I learnt to look for them myself and not get into trouble when she checked them.'

He said nothing, just stared thoughtfully at the phial.

Then she gave a theatrical start. 'Looks like three fingers, don't it, sir?' she said forgetting to call him Officer Grey.

He did not correct her. He turned the phial around, still keeping his finger and thumb in the same position.

'Perhaps his little finger didn't go on to it,' he said after a minute.

'But the first finger mark should be opposite to the thumb, that's right, ain't it?' Sarah looked at his face as she said those words and saw him slowly nod. 'And that last one looks like a little finger, don't it? Look, you can see how small and narrow it is. Looks like the first finger is missing.'

'Pretend to put your hand around it,' he said slowly. 'Don't touch it. Just go near to it.'

Sarah curved her hand, putting her thumb near to the thumb mark. Her forefinger was just opposite to a place where no mark showed, but the other three fingers were near to the marks on the glass. Once again, he nodded.

'Looks as though you're right,' he said. 'Well, well, well, three fingers. That's interesting.'

'Grey!' came a shout. 'Grey, where the blazes have you got to?'

Officer Grey straightened up. 'Keep this to yourself,' he said. To her dismay he slipped the phial into his pocket and strode off. Then he came back and handed her a sixpence.

'Keep this to yourself,' he repeated in a low voice and then raised it to shout, 'Coming, sir.'

Sarah went on with her work, bringing a damp cloth to various grimy places that showed up by the white limelight. She wondered whether to turn it off, but decided that it was none of her business. Officer Grey should have done that. As she worked she kept an ear open for Alfie and when she heard a faint noise, she picked up her duster, brooms, bucket and mop and made her way backstage. She opened her mouth to tell him about her discovery, but she could not do so. There was a sound of footsteps coming down the aisle, then climbing up the stairs that led to the stage.

Alfie melted away once more and Sarah climbed on a chair and vigorously began to dust the top of a tall cupboard.

'Can you see that? Those limelights are good for the actors but they don't give much light on high.' The man who had come in was dressed in overalls and carried a candle. He raised it up high so that the top of the cupboard was illuminated. 'There, is that better?' he asked.

It was a beautiful voice, deep, musical, as smooth as hot chocolate. A voice for ladies to dream about!

But the face that Sarah saw by the light of the candle was a nightmare, slashed from side to side, puckered and with lumpy white scar tissue.

Sarah stared at him and then hurriedly looked away. This must be John Osborne, the man whose face had been slashed by Harry Booth. She caught her breath in sympathy. What must it be like to see a face like that in the looking glass, to see the horror in the eyes of everyone who met him, to know that he could never again play the part of a hero at the theatre?

And it was Harry Booth who had done that to him.

Had John Osborne taken a terrible revenge on the man who had mutilated him for life? Especially if he considered that Harry Booth had done it on purpose . . .

Was she looking into the face of Harry Booth's murderer?

CHAPTER 12

BETRAYED

As he left the cellar, Tom felt furious. He walked along the foggy street, kicking at lamp-posts and muttering to himself. That Sarah was just too bossy! What right had she to order him about? Come to that, what right had Alfie to order him to do things? Why should he do what any of them told him? He was fed up. Fed up with being hungry, fed up with being the one who was given all the worst jobs to do. Things hadn't been too bad when his friend Charlie had lived with the gang, but now Charlie had gone back to the countryside where he had been born.

Tom stopped at a shop and gazed longingly in. It

was a dairy shop, full of huge round cheeses, tempting slices of each of them lying on wooden platters, great brick-sized lumps of fresh butter, salted butter – every kind of butter, with small cubes for housewives and cooks to taste and choose. There were custard pies on tin plates and milk jellies wobbling on others.

But the shop was empty of customers and the shopkeeper, a large man with ginger whiskers, was standing there towering over his cheeses and glaring at Tom as he peeped in. There was no hope of stealing anything.

It was the same at Covent Garden market. The freezing fog had made everyone head for home quickly. There was no press of people, no crowds where a boy who had just stolen an apple pie from a stall could hide himself. Shopping was almost over for the day. Many of the stallholders had begun to put away their goods. And every one of them was on the alert when they saw a ragged, barefoot boy approach.

Perhaps Sammy had been luckier, thought Tom. He stopped for a moment. He had determined that he wasn't going to do what he was told, but now he was inclined to search for his cousin. He wasn't obeying Sarah, he told himself. It just made sense to find Sammy. The combination of being blind and having a good singing voice often worked when nothing else did; there might be a capful of money by the time that he found Sammy. He would tell Sammy that Alfie had ordered him to bring home some sausages. At the thought of them, Tom's mouth watered.

There was still no sign of Sammy outside either of the two usual churches, St Martin-in the Fields and St Mary-le-Strand, so Tom began to ask passers-by. There were a few more people around – clerks finishing a day's work, shopkeepers taking in boards from the wet pavements, but no one had noticed a blind boy and a hairy dog. Tom stood and thought. The chances were that no one on the Strand had stopped to listen to Sammy. So what would Sammy do? He hadn't gone home, so where had he gone?

Tom wandered along Fleet Street. No sign of Sammy there. He tried asking a few of the newspapermen dashing in and out of their offices, but they brushed him away – like I was a bluebottle, he thought to himself indignantly. Next he went up through Aldwych and along Drury Lane. There was no sign of Sammy anywhere, but there was an elderly well-dressed lady standing alone outside a greengrocer's shop. Tom approached her with a hand outstretched.

'Please ma'am, would you spare a penny,' he whined. 'I've had no food for nearly two days.'

'Get off with you,' she shouted. 'Go home and wash your face and get yourself a job and don't go preying on a defenceless person like myself. Officer!' her voice rose to a shrill note as she beckoned to a nearby policeman.

'I'm going,' muttered Tom furiously, running as fast as he could in the opposite direction to the policeman, down Drury Lane and back into the Strand.

I'll try Smithfield, he thought.

It made sense for Sammy to go there. Bad weather would not stop people going to Smithfield. The meat had to be bought and butchered and taken to the shops, cut up into neat little joints and chops, wrapped in brown paper and delivered by the butchers' boys to the homes of the toffs.

Smithfield was a place full of queues where the shoppers would be glad to pass their time listening to a song and would spare their halfpence, pence, groats and sixpences to reward the singer. It was a dangerous place for a blind boy – Alfie would never have suggested that Sammy go there on his own. You needed to have eyes in the back of your head to avoid being trampled by cattle, pigs or even sheep at Smithfield. But Sammy would know that they were all desperate for food and might go to take his chance there.

Worth a try, thought Tom to himself and he set off east towards the meat market.

Tom had never been to church, but once he had listened to an outdoor sermon about hell. He had been just passing by, but the words had grabbed him and he stayed, open-mouthed at the descriptions of what happened to the wicked after they had died. He had had nightmares about hell for months and was reminded of it just now. Smithfield was a hell: a hell of blood and foam and death. As he watched, he saw a child go down, slipping in the ankle-deep river of liquid animal muck. Tom turned away quickly from the screams. There was nothing he could do. He was sorry now that he had come.

And then he thought of Mutsy.

Of course, Mutsy would steer Sammy away from the terrible danger and he would guide him to the stalls at the outside of the market. As soon as he thought of that Tom began to hurry. Now he guessed where Sammy might be. The chestnut seller at Smithfield was quite a friend to the gang. He had invited Sammy to come and sing at his stall as often as he liked. You only had to say 'chestnuts' to Mutsy and he would lead you straight to one of those men with a portable iron brazier who roasted chestnuts on street corners. Mutsy had got to love chestnuts and so did Tom. His mouth began to water at the thought.

And that's where Sammy was. Tom could hear the high, sweet voice singing as he came nearer to the well-remembered place. There were a few people around and already the cap on the ground glinted with copper coins and one piece of silver.

Mutsy looked across at Tom and wagged his tail hard. Tom grinned back. This was good. Just beside Sammy was a tin plate of cooling chestnuts. When the song ended he would join his cousin and the dog. Sammy would share the chestnuts with him.

And then a hand came down hard on his shoulder. A voice spoke in his ear. 'Do you know the owner of that dog, boy?'

Behind him was a man, a small fat man, warmly dressed, collar turned up, hat pulled over his eyes, hands gloved . . .

Tom stared at the man suspiciously. What was he after?

'I saw that dog with another boy the last time, a dark-haired boy. I'd like to have a word with that chap,' said the voice. 'Could you take me to him?'

Tom hesitated, looking across at Sammy. Alfie was on the run. Was this a policeman after him, wanting to arrest him?

'Are you hungry, boy?' the voice went on. Tom twisted around, but the hat was pulled well down. He couldn't see the man's face, but he thought the cloak and trousers didn't look like a policeman.

'Yes, sir,' he said, and for the third time that day his mouth watered.

'There's a pie shop over there,' said the man, still keeping his hand on Tom's shoulder.

Tom gave one glance at Sammy. He had just started a new song. Tom knew it well. It was a song with many verses. He would be back before it was finished.

The pie shop was very near – only a few steps away. The man let go of Tom and marched up to the counter. 'Steak and kidney pie,' he said.

Tom almost felt faint as the pie was slid on to the plate. His eyes were fixed on it as it came towards him. The man had to speak twice before he heard him properly.

'I said you'll get the pie when you tell me where the boy is hiding.' That was what the man said.

And Tom heard his own voice saying, 'He dressed

up as a clown and he's hiding in Covent Garden Theatre.'

And then he grabbed the pie and started to wolf it down, scared that it would be taken from him before he had eaten it.

But when he finished licking the plate and looked up, the man had gone.

Gone where? To Covent Garden Theatre?

Suddenly he vomited, spewing up all of that lovely pie. His stomach had rejected the food that he had wanted so badly.

He had betrayed his cousin.

And now it was all for nothing.

CHAPTER 13

THE
HUNT

Sarah was the first to see the policeman. She was busily rubbing away at the chairs in the orchestra pit below the stage while Alfie lay on his stomach beside the drums and they talked to each other in whispers, discussing possibilities. 'John Osborne is the most likely,' Alfie had just said in a low voice when Sarah hushed him.

It wasn't one of the Scotland Yard policemen; they didn't wear uniform. This was a local 'bobby' or 'peeler' from Bow Street Police Station. The man was too far away to see the number on his collar, but Sarah could see the navy blue uniform, the shiny hat, the high leather boots – Wellingtons, they called them.

He was far away, but both of them heard his words distinctly.

'Have you got a boy here? A boy called Alfie Sykes? Wanted for questioning about the murder last night?'

'Boy, I've got no boy here.' The manager sounded peevish and bad-tempered. No wonder, thought Alfie. If his theatre was losing money and he was facing bankruptcy, the last thing he wanted was police swarming all over the place.

'We've had a tip-off,' persisted the Bow Street bobby. 'Our informant says that the boy dressed up as a clown. Member of the public told us. Not ten minutes ago. Came to Bow Street Police Station to lay information.'

'I didn't engage any boy . . . at least . . .' The manager had begun by shouting, but now his voice tailed off.

'But what, sir? You did engage some clowns earlier, didn't you?' This was a different voice. Sarah could see the two policemen from Scotland Yard come out from the door at the back. They left the door open behind them and now all four men could be seen plainly in the light that came from behind them.

The manager removed his tall hat and scratched his head. 'There was a small fellow – with two other clowns, he was. Perhaps he could have been a boy, now that I come to think of it.'

'Well, that's easily settled.' The first Scotland Yard policeman seemed to have taken over. 'Are the clowns here?'

'Some of them are hanging around, I suppose.' The manager sounded impatient. It must be getting near to the time of the performance, thought Sarah. He had a note of anger in his voice when he shouted, 'Jimmy, if there are any of those new clowns back there tell them to come here.'

'Can I get away, Sarah?' Alfie kept his whisper down very low. He knew how sounds could travel in this tall-roofed building.

'No,' muttered Sarah, as she polished frantically. 'Stay where you are.' He was in the worst possible place, trapped in the tiny pit, but there was no possibility of him climbing out without being seen. Just that very moment a man started to walk down the side aisle with a long pole, switching on the little gas nozzles and lighting them up. Bit by bit the whole of the theatre was becoming as bright as a summer's day.

Alfie, from his place by the drums, saw the light and knew that now only an extraordinary piece of luck could save him.

The clowns were coming out – he could hear the

sound of shuffling feet. They all walked like clowns, off stage as well as on stage, he thought, trying to be calm.

Wait for the moment, and then run for it, he said to himself. He wondered whether the exit doors at the side of the theatre would be open, but decided not. They would never leave those unlocked in case someone sneaked in there during the day. No, the only exit would be through one of the two main doors, the front door or the back door – and each of these had a man in front of it.

'Hey, you two, what are your names?' The manager's voice was high and impatient.

'Joey and Lucky, sir.'

'Where's the third man in your act? The little fellow – where's he gone?'

There was a silence for a moment and then Joey spoke. 'Don't know, sir. He just joined in. You saw yourself. He ran on to the stage and joined us. Wouldn't know him from Adam.'

'Could he have been a boy?'

There was a long silence and then Joey said, 'Perhaaaaps,' drawing out the word in a theatrical way.

The Scotland Yard policeman made an impatient sound. 'We'll have to search the place. Come on, you men, you can help. A reward of one pound to the man who finds him.'

That got them going. Alfie listened in dismay. No more shuffling – those clowns started thundering down the aisles, rattling at seats, banging doors, calling out excitedly. Who could blame them? A shilling for a night's performance and a whole pound just for finding a boy hiding in the theatre!

Alfie bit his lip. A tiny corner of him regretted that he would never get the chance, now, to go on the boards at Covent Garden Theatre and hear an audience laugh and clap at his performance, but most of his mind was occupied with plans of how to get away from the hunt.

'Sarah,' he whispered urgently. 'Is there any way that you could close the curtains on the stage for a few minutes?'

Sarah did not reply. She was clever, Sarah was. Someone might be looking at her. He was sure that she had heard him and would do her best. While he was waiting, Alfie discarded the ragged old cloak, the bowler hat and the too-long trousers. All of these would slow him down. Impatiently, he shoved them all under the drum platform. He was going to strip off the waistcoat too, but it began to tear as he endeavoured to pull the fragile material from over his bulky, ragged jacket. He remembered Betty's fear of her grandmother and decided to leave it for the moment. He would ease it off later when he had more time and shove it into his pocket. He spat on his hands and scrubbed at the paint on his face and lips and at the lamp-black around his eyes. Now he wouldn't attract too much attention if he managed to escape on to the streets.

A second later he heard a heavy tread and then the voice of the manager. 'You haven't seen a boy hiding anywhere, have you, girl?'

'No, sir,' said Sarah earnestly. 'He's definitely not backstage. I'd have seen him. I've been washing and dusting and polishing up there for the past half an hour.'

'And she's very thorough at her work.' That was the second Scotland Yard man, Officer Grey. He sounded amused by Sarah. He lifted his voice now and shouted, 'Try the boxes, lads. No point in going backstage. Flush him out. Hey, you, hurry up with those lamps! The more light we have, the quicker we'll find him.'

'Please, sir,' said Sarah. She was addressing the manager, now, thought Alfie. 'Would you mind if I closed the curtains on the stage, sir? I want to get the dust off them.' She brandished a feather duster on its long bamboo. Alfie could see it waving. He hoped this would work. Everything was getting very bright. It was time that he got a better hiding place. He shrank further back into the shadow of the drum.

'Yes, yes, go on, but take care. Those curtains are new.' The manager sounded more irritable by the minute.

Alfie waited. Sarah had gone; he knew that. He wished that he could see whether the curtain was closed but it would be madness to raise his head. It seemed a long, long time before he heard something, but when he did the noise was unmistakable. The heavy curtains were swishing across the stage.

Instantly Alfie acted. In a second he was up the steps. He pushed the trapdoor open and flung himself out of the hole and on to the stage.

But as soon as he landed a figure moved from the wings and a voice spoke. 'I thought you might do that again!' And Alfie looked up and saw the manager, who reached down, grabbed a fistful of Betty's waistcoat and held Alfie tight.

'You murdered one of my actors,' he said. 'You'll hang for this!

CHAPTER 14

HUNTED DOWN

Alfie froze. There was no escape for him now.

The manager raised his voice triumphantly. 'I've got him!'

There was a sudden silence. Feet stopped pounding. No one spoke. Alfie stood perfectly still; he took a deep breath, inhaling power into his muscles.

Now was the last moment for escape. Alfie eyed the gantry, the framework of iron bars which criss-crossed the stage above his head. He had seen men swing down from it, hand over hand, and land in the centre of the stage.

The curtains were jerked back impatiently by a Scotland Yard policeman.

'Ah, Inspector Cutting!' the manager said with satisfaction. He started to drag Alfie over towards the policeman who was pounding up the steps to the stage, but Alfie was ready, every fibre in his body alert. He exerted all his force to wrench himself free. And, as he had expected, the much-mended silk waistcoat ripped in half, leaving the manager holding a torn piece of material.

Suddenly free, Alfie grabbed the curtain, hauled himself up, seized the lowest bar of the gantry, swung his body and hooked his knees around the metal. Now he was above the manager's head.

'Shoot him, shoot him!' shouted the manager.

'After him, men!' yelled the Scotland Yard policeman and four of the younger clowns started to climb across the gantry – two in front of him, one to the right of him and one behind, with Alfie directly above the centre of the stage.

Alfie had not expected this. He had forgotten that lots of clowns were acrobats, also. These four certainly were at home on the vast framework of iron bars. It was like a nightmare, up there in the strange, hot dimness, surrounded by grinning mouths, painted-on faces . . . Trapped! He could not go back or go forward.

'Don't move, boy, or I'll shoot!' roared Inspector Cutting, pointing his pistol at Alfie. 'Go on, men. He's only a kid. Grab him!'

Alfie waited, crouched and tense. He grasped the bar above him and allowed his feet to swing clear. The first man that approached would get kicked in a very painful place, he promised himself grimly.

'Arrest that girl. Look! She's trying to sneak over towards him.' The manager sounded hysterical. 'She's an accomplice! She was screening him from us in the pit and then she drew the curtain to give him a chance to escape by the trapdoor.'

'Arrest her, Officer Grey,' said Inspector Cutting.

As all eyes turned towards Sarah, Alfie looked quickly around.

Tied to one end of the gantry he saw a strong rope, looped up to keep it out of the way. It was used, he supposed, for actors to suddenly swoop down on to the stage – but Alfie did not want to go back down on to the stage, with its fiercely white limelight.

He looked out across the body of the theatre. The boxes, where the rich and famous took their seats, lined both sidewalls of the Covent Garden Theatre, each with its own gas lamp. Almost all of the boxes on the left-hand side had been lit by now, but those on the right-hand side were still in darkness. If only he could get over there, get into one of them, he could duck from one box to another and escape.

But was the rope long enough?

Alfie took hold of the end of the rope, waiting for the right moment. Everyone was watching him and the four clowns were getting dangerously close.

On the other hand, the nearer they were, the less likely it became that the police inspector from Scotland Yard would shoot. Alfie made himself wait another few nerve-racking seconds.

'We'll get him!' shrieked one clown.

'We'll split the pound with you and your partner!' screamed another.

Alfie clutched the rope and looked out across the immense space between himself and the first of the boxes – the royal box where Queen Victoria had sat . . . was it only last night?

And then he jumped.

He swooped through the air, his legs kicking wildly. His bare feet met the edge of the box, tried desperately to hook over the side and failed.

He swung back and felt himself falling . . . and

crashed back down on to the stage. There was a tremendous thud; some boards with painted scenes upon them smashed to the ground. The manager swore, the clowns shouted from overhead, the inspector called out an order to 'give yourself up in the name of the law', but Alfie was on the move again.

Picking himself up from the ground, still clutching the rope with an energy born of despair, he leapt up and swung out past the manager, past the inspector, past Sarah . . .

This time he landed on a seat just in the middle of the pit.

The inspector fired a shot. Alfie ducked down and it whistled over his head. He crawled along the floor, squeezing under the seats and moving rapidly from row to row. His mind was working furiously. How could he get out of this building? The Bow Street constable was guarding the door at the top of the aisle. He looked under the seats and could see some legs walking up the aisle in between the seats. He knew what was happening – small black shoes and skirt beside large shoes and a frock coat.

Sarah, her bucket, mop and brooms abandoned, was walking up the aisle beside a Scotland Yard policeman. He hoped she would be able to talk her way out of trouble, but there was nothing that he could do to help her. He had enough problems himself. He risked a quick peep above the seat.

The inspector was walking up the middle aisle, holding his gun at the ready and scanning each row. The manager was beside him, shouting at the lamplighter to hurry up and get the rest of the boxes lit up. Alfie curled up under a seat, tearing off the remains of the colourful silk waistcoat and the white shirt and tucking it under him. Now he would be hard to see as his own clothes were the same colour as the grimy surface of the pit. He made himself lie with his face turned inwards and cautiously smeared some of the dust and grit from the floor over the remains of Betty's face paint.

'He can't have got out!' The inspector sounded furious.

'No, sir,' the anxious voice of the Bow Street policeman came down the aisle. 'No possibility, sir! Not even a mouse could get by me, here.'

'Sir!' That was one of the clowns, Alfie knew. He was talking in the professional squeaky voice. 'Me and Toby can help you. I'll claim that pound from you, sir, in a few minutes, I will if he's still in the building. Wait and see if I do!'

There was an excited bark and Alfie's heart fell. He knew those little dogs that clowns used. Very well trained for all sorts of tricks! But this was a job that any dog could do.

'Rats, Toby! Rats!' The clown squeaked the words and the dog squealed with excitement.

And Toby came skidding down the aisle, running in and out of the rows, jumping on seats, sniffing so loudly that he could be heard from yards away.

And then he gave a triumphant bark.

Alfie felt a cold, wet nose against his bare leg. He put out his hand reluctantly and stroked the dog, feeling the tiny, thin tail wagging frantically.

It was all up with him.

He could hear the thunderous footsteps of one policeman in the row behind him and another running rapidly along the row in front of him.

He stood up and silently held out his hands as the Bow Street constable, at a signal from the inspector, slipped handcuffs over his wrists.

'It's Newgate prison for you, my lad,' said Inspector Cutting.

CHAPTER 15

LIFE OR DEATH

Sarah was still with Officer Grey in the foyer of the theatre when Alfie was led out. He didn't look at her and she did not look at him. She had just sworn solemnly to the Scotland Yard man that she had never seen Alfie before in her life.

'And a good, hard-working girl like you would know how wrong, how very wrong, and sinful it is to tell a lie,' he had said, looking at her closely.

'Yes, of course.' She had tried to throw a great note of sincerity into her voice and he had nodded.

He seemed quite a nice fellow, she thought – educated, too, from the way that he spoke. But someone like him wouldn't – couldn't – ever understand the life that people like she and Alfie had to lead: the continual need to lie and even to steal in order to keep alive. On the cruel streets of London where no one cared about poor children any more than they cared about stray dogs, sin wasn't important: survival was everything.

'Well, off you go then,' he said. 'You'd better scarper. Don't let me see you around here again, or I'll be in trouble. With a bit of luck, the boss will forget all about you.'

She nodded, hesitated, looked back at the theatre. 'No use my going back for my money, I suppose,' she said, endeavouring to keep her tone light and to prevent a note of bitterness from coming to the surface.

The police officer grinned. 'I wouldn't if I were you,' he said. 'Here you are.' He put his hand in his pocket, took out a sixpence and gave it to her. He gave a cautious look around. There was nobody near, but he still lowered his voice so that only she could hear him saying, 'I owe you something for noticing the finger marks. It would be interesting if it turns out to be a man with a missing finger that murdered that actor, wouldn't it? Do my career no end of good if I could pin it on someone. It's obvious that the boy was working for someone. What interest would a street boy like that have in murdering an actor? No, he was paid to go on stage and distract attention while our friend with the missing finger made his getaway.'

What about Alfie? wondered Sarah. He didn't have a missing finger, so why was it all right for him to be arrested? But she didn't dare say her thoughts aloud. Even a decent man like Officer Grey would have little concern for a street boy. She nodded, smiled and left him with a few grateful words. It was nice of him to give her sixpence – you could buy a large loaf of bread for fourpence so that should be enough for the three hungry boys at Bow Street.

Life for Alfie and his gang was a matter of surviving from day to day. But how would they manage now that their leader had been taken off to prison?

CHAPTER 16

AN OLD FRIEND

Sarah walked slowly down the steps from the theatre. A sob escaped her. She clenched her hands. Crying was stupid; she knew that. She had to think of something to do. It was all up to her now. But what was she to do?

'Here! You're little Sarah, aren't you? Little Sarah from the Foundling Hospital, that's right, ain't it?'

Sarah shook the tears from her eyes and looked up. A very tall girl with masses of golden, curly hair stood above her. She was five or six years older than Sarah – probably about eighteen. There was something familiar about the voice – and about the hair, too.

'You *are* Sarah!' said the girl. 'Don't you remember

me – Rosa? Don't you remember me brushing your hair?'

'I remember,' said Sarah with a smile. 'You've changed, Rosa.' Rosa had been one of the big girls in the Foundling Hospital for abandoned children at Coram Fields. She had been very kind to Sarah, playing with her as if she was a doll, doing her hair but also making sure that none of the other older girls stole Sarah's food.

'Well, you haven't changed,' said Rosa cheerfully. 'Still the same little skinny Sarah. I'd know those big green eyes anywhere. You haven't grown much, either, have you? What are you doing with yourself these days?'

'I'm in service,' said Sarah, trying to sound cheerful. 'I've a job as a scullery maid.'

'Skivvy, eh – I tried that for a while. No future in it. Then a gentleman got me a place in the chorus here at Covent Garden and now I'm a leading lady, if you please.'

'Oh, you were in the play last night! I saw it. I didn't recognise you!'

'Didn't get a chance to do my solo act,' said Rosa, 'what with that murder and all. You see'd that murder, did you?'

Sarah nodded and then thought of Alfie. Her eyes began to fill up again.

'What's the matter, sweetheart? Are you hungry? Come on, we'll have a cup of hot chocolate at the stall there. I'm supposed to be meeting my young man, Francis, but he can wait.'

Sarah sat up with a start. What was it that Alfie had said about Francis Fairburn, and Harry Booth taking his girlfriend away from him? Rosa must be the girlfriend! Now she could learn more about both men. She waited until Rosa had pressed the mug of hot chocolate into her hand then followed her meekly as Rosa moved away from the counter and sat down at a small table beside a brazier of hot coals.

'Oh, Rosa, is Francis Fairburn your young man? He's ever so handsome,' said Sarah. She hadn't ever seen Francis Fairburn, but even at twelve, Rosa had been eager to talk about handsome boys, and Sarah wanted to encourage her to speak.

'He's mad about me,' said Rosa with a giggle. 'For a while, Harry Booth – you know, the bloke that was murdered – for a while I went out with him, but then I went back to Francis Fairburn.'

'Which did you like best?' asked Sarah. It was easy to put on an innocent air with Rosa. As they sat there, side by side, sipping their hot chocolate, it was like being back in the Foundling Hospital again.

'Oh, definitely Francis,' said Rosa. 'Harry Booth was a nasty piece of work. That's a terrible thing to say about someone who's dead, but he was always sneaking around and finding out things about people and then asking for money to keep quiet about it. No, I soon went back to Francis.' She sipped her drink and gave a half-giggle. 'It's a terrible thing to say,' she repeated, 'but me and Francis were cuddling and kissing in the wings just at that very moment that Harry Booth was killed.'

This seemed to put Francis Fairburn out of the picture, Sarah thought. Rosa wouldn't bother lying to her little friend from the old days.

'Who do you think did it, Rosa?' she asked. 'I heard someone say when I was cleaning the floor in there that a man called John Osborne did it.'

Rosa pursed up her red lips. 'Could be,' she admitted. 'But they say that someone sneaked in and put poison in the glass without anyone noticing it. Well, if you ever see'd John Osborne, you'll never forget his face. Someone would have noticed him. No, I think it was probably one of them clowns. With the costume and all that make-up you can't tell one from the other. They was all lined up there and moving about and changing places. No one would have noticed one of them slipping behind the curtains.' She looked carefully at Sarah and then said sharply, 'Here, why are you so interested?'

'Everyone is interested in that murder,' said Sarah, trying to smile, but Rosa continued to look at her suspiciously.

'Don't you lie to me, young Sarah,' she said with authority. 'Come on now, tell the truth. You're holding something back, ain't you?'

Sarah twisted her fingers together, trying to make up her mind. Her own mother had abandoned her when she was a tiny baby – left her outside the Foundling Hospital – and Rosa was the nearest thing to a mother that she had ever had.

And she sounded just like a mother now, thought Sarah. She tried to give a casual smile but then the tears welled up again.

'Oh, Rosa,' she said, taking a large gulp of the hot chocolate in order to prevent a sob escaping, 'the police have arrested a friend of mine, Alfie – the boy that ran on stage when Harry Booth died. Alfie didn't do it, but now they've taken him off to prison. I have to find out who really did kill Harry Booth. Oh, Rosa, you know all of these people. Will you help me? Please, Rosa, for old times' sake.'

Rosa took a long drink of the hot chocolate, keeping both eyes fixed on Sarah's face as she drank. Eventually she drained the last drops, put down the mug, looked carefully all around and then said quietly, 'I'll ask around to see who was near to the curtains at the time, but I'll be keeping one thing in my mind, and you remember it too, young Sarah. Whoever killed Harry Booth will be having both ears open to see if anyone is asking questions.'

Sarah nodded but Rosa hadn't finished. Her voice sank even lower as she added slowly, 'They say in St Giles that no one kills only once. The more you kill, the easier it gets – that's what they say.'

CHAPTER 17

TREACHERY UNCOVERED

The fog was still thick when Sarah came out of Covent Garden market. She hurried along Bow Street, feeling her way along the wall, keeping to the inside of the pavement. The few horses and cabs that were out were blundering around, unable to see the road and occasionally running up against pedestrians. The gas lamps cast no light on the pavements, but were just misty globes of glimmering yellow in the darkness above their heads.

Sarah stopped at a shop and bought a loaf of bread and some milk. She felt a great sense of responsibility for the gang now that Alfie was gone. He was always careful to stop them from drinking water. His mother had died of cholera – a disease which had ripped through the neighbourhood from drinking water poisoned with the sewage that had seeped into it.

The fire was glowing through the dirty window of the boys' cellar. Suddenly she found her face wet with tears. Would Alfie ever come home again? She dashed the wetness from her cheeks, swallowed hard and then rapped on the door. Sammy was back, anyway; Mutsy's deep bark had sounded as she came down the steps and now he was sniffing so loudly that it almost seemed as though he wanted to draw her in through the door on one deep intake of breath.

Jack was absent, but Tom was there, a very subdued Tom who seemed almost disappointed to see her. Perhaps he was still sulking after her rough words earlier. She decided to ignore him and talk to Sammy.

'So Tom found you, then, Sammy, is that right?' Sarah sat down beside him. How would the blind boy manage without his brother? The thought would not go from her mind and she bit her lip to prevent a sob.

'Nah,' said Sammy in his peaceful way, 'Mutsy and I got home by ourselves.'

'I looked every place,' said Tom defensively. There was something strange about his tone. Sarah glanced at him, but the fire was low and the room almost in darkness.

'Where were you, then, Sammy?' asked Sarah.

'Me and Mutsy went to Smithfield. I had to leave the Strand. There was a bloke, some sort of toff, I reckon – the same fellow as gave Alfie the tickets, I'd say, because he spoke the way that Alfie said, sort of disguising his voice – funny sort of voice. Well, he kept asking me where Alfie was and if I could lead him to my brother. I reckoned he was up to no good so I whispered to Mutsy to bring me to Smithfield – to throw him off the scent, like.'

'Did he follow you, pester you any more?'

'He followed me all right,' agreed Sammy. 'He had me by the arm, but then the chestnut seller came up and asked me to sing. He let go me then. He didn't ask any more questions, but I could smell him there for a long time – watching me . . .'

'What did he smell like?' Sarah found nothing strange in this; she knew Sammy's special powers.

'Like I said, a toff – cigars, leather gloves, good cloak, good wool in it.' Sammy was quite casual.

There was a faint sound from Tom. Sarah turned to

him. 'Are you all right, Tom?' He had crept over and was now sitting on the stone edge of the fireplace. She noticed that he was shivering. 'Are you feeling sick?' she asked with concern. By the light of the fire she could see that he looked white and hollowed-eyed.

'Have you had anything to eat?' she asked.

Tom nodded, suddenly seeming younger than his usual self. 'A pie,' he said, shuddering. 'I sicked it all up.'

'A pie!' she echoed with astonishment. 'Where did you get a pie?'

He hesitated, shrugged and looked back into the flames before answering. 'Someone gave it to me, same as someone gave Sammy a plate of chestnuts.' His tone was bitter.

'How did you know that I had chestnuts?' Sammy sounded mildly surprised.

'Saw you, didn't I?' Tom tried to sound aggressive, but the teeth were rattling in his mouth.

'Was you in Smithfield, then?' Sammy sounded mildly curious, but Sarah immediately became suspicious.

'Who gave you the pie?' she asked, trying to keep her voice even and indifferent.

He shrugged again. Always trying to act the tough

man, Sarah thought. Alfie was a bit hard on him, perhaps. In Alfie's eyes, Tom should be like Sammy: sensible and hard-working. They were much of an age, but Tom seemed younger than Sammy in all sorts of ways. Alfie resented Tom, had always resented him. Alfie's mother had taken her nephews Jack and Tom in when their mother had died, and it seemed she had always favoured Tom over Jack, and even over her own two sons sometimes. According to Alfie, Tom had never given up thinking that he was something special.

Sarah thought hard. Perhaps she could get the truth out of him by acting a motherly part.

'Who gave it to you, Tom?' she said in a low, sympathetic tone. She reached out her hand and stroked his hair.

He moved away, but she sensed that he had been pleased by her gesture. He probably missed a bit of mothering.

'Swear you won't tell Alfie,' he said and she nodded.

'I got it from the cove who wanted to know where Alfie was,' he admitted. He took a quick look at her face and then said in a swaggering fashion. 'I didn't tell him nothing, of course. I took the pie and bolted.'

'Of course,' said Sarah in a soothing manner. There was no point in saying anything else. She needed to get as much information as possible. If Alfie was ever to get out of Newgate, they would need to find out everything about the possible killer of Harry Booth.

'So he gave you the pie and it didn't agree with you, was that it?' she asked softly. Sammy was listening, she thought. He had not turned his face towards them, but his whole body was alert. Mutsy also had not slumped down by the fire, but was sitting bolt upright, with his large intelligent head facing them.

'That's right,' agreed Tom, sounding a bit more cheerful. 'It was a great pie. If you smelt it, Sarah!'

'But you couldn't keep it down,' said Sarah. 'Perhaps it was bad, was it?'

'Perhaps,' agreed Tom. But then his face darkened and he looked away from her.

Sarah took a deep breath. She had to know the truth. 'I suppose you felt upset that you told him about Alfie's disguise,' she said, keeping her voice calm.

Tom stared at her. Sammy did not move, but Mutsy shifted his position, fixed his eyes on the blind boy's face and put his paw on his lap. The dog sensed the blind boy's distress. Sammy was prepared for the worst; Sarah knew that. She could go ahead and get the rest of the truth out of this stupid boy, Tom.

'And he gave you a pie just for telling him about Alfie dressing up as a clown?' she said, trying to make sure that her voice had a note of disbelief in it.

'That's right,' said Tom. 'I didn't think there was any harm in it.' He spoke with a self-righteous air which made her long to box his ears.

'What did this toff look like?' she said, and then, when he just shrugged, she said sharply, 'Come on, Tom, Alfie is in trouble, we must do our best to help him.'

'That's Jack,' said Tom and immediately bounded to his feet and rushed over to the door, anxious to get away from Sarah.

'All right, Tom?' Jack seemed to sense that something was wrong. He stayed a moment peering into his younger brother's face and then hauled the quarter-filled sack of coal over to the fireplace. He was stone-cold and shivering. His bare feet were swollen with chilblains – his hands too, with monstrous fingers, where the knuckles were lost within the puffy red flesh. Sarah looked at him with pity. He was only a little more than a year older than Tom, but, like Alfie, Jack had been born with this sense of responsibility which made him take care of his younger brother.

'Take my seat,' she said to Jack. 'Don't put those feet of yours too near the fire. That will make them worse. I wish I had some ointment to put on them. They look really bad.'

'They're all right. I had to hang around the shoreline for ages. In this weather, every bit of coal seemed to have been picked up – even though I went into the river right up to the top of me legs. In the end, I had to wait for the evening boats.' Jack's voice was hoarse. He started to rub his itching toes, but then stopped himself.

'Where's Alfie?' Jack looked all around. He looked worried.

Sarah took a deep breath. 'I'm afraid there is bad news about Alfie,' she said. 'There were posters out saying that he was wanted for questioning about the murder. Scotland Yard were after him. Alfie dressed up as a clown – he thought he could pass as a small man acting the part of a clown and he went into the theatre.' She paused and then said, picking her words carefully, 'He might have got away with it, but someone laid information at Bow Street Police Station. They told the whole story – don't know who did it –

but whoever they were, they knew that Alfie had dressed up as a clown.' She hesitated, but Jack had to know the truth. 'The police took Alfie away.'

Jack slumped down in front of the fire and put his head into his hands. Sammy was silent and Tom's face drained of colour.

'Where did they take him?' Jack asked hoarsely.

'To Newgate,' said Sarah unsteadily. I won't tell him about Tom yet, she thought. One piece of bad news at a time.

'Newgate!' Jack was on his feet. His croaky voice broke on the word. He coughed, gulped and looked at her imploringly. 'What are we going to do, Sarah? There's only two ways out of Newgate: transportation or the gallows.'

Sarah swallowed a lump in her throat. He was right. Those were the sentences handed down to the prisoners at Newgate.

A life of hard labour in a distant country, maybe Australia – a year's voyage from London.

Or death at the end of a rope.

CHAPTER 18

NEWGATE

Alfie's brain was numb. He could neither hear nor speak. He felt himself pushed and dragged by the Scotland Yard inspector. Shoved into a cab.

Then pulled out of the cab.

Awkward, stumbling.

Cuffs on his wrists and irons on his legs.

The cabman's voice – 'I go no further, governor. Not through Temple Bar. The fog's too bad. You'll just have to walk the rest of the way.'

Curses.

A few blows. The Scotland Yard man venting his anger at having to walk.

Nothing much. Alfie had had worse.

He just went on.

Doggedly putting one leg in front of the other, dragging the heavy irons, holding his manacled hands out in front of him. He had a curious sense of being unable to balance, of needing his hands free to feel the way through this fog. But the Scotland Yard man, Inspector Cutting, had a tight grip on his collar. He was being pushed forward, down Fleet Street, going step by step to Newgate.

And now they were in Newgate Street. The iron was burning through his ankles, rubbing the skin raw, but he hardly felt it. His arms were stiff, but he hardly felt that either.

At the prison gate, the inspector spoke to the lodge keeper and a turnkey arrived, the man that looked after the prisoners. He took Alfie by the arm, marched him down the passageways. There must have been about a hundred of these stone passages! Continually they stopped while the turnkey took yet another enormous key from his bunch and opened yet another gate. The walls were dripping with green slime and the stench was almost unbearable. The covered lantern held by the turnkey made their shadows look like giant apparitions on the wall and the noise of his boots on the flagstones echoed like the beating of a giant hammer.

'Like to see something?' said the turnkey and Alfie started to hear the voice booming around and bouncing from stone wall to stone wall.

'Yes,' he said. He didn't suppose it mattered whether he said yes or no; the turnkey could do as he pleased with his manacled and shackled prisoner.

'That's the condemned cell,' whispered the turnkey after a moment. His whisper sounded more threatening than any yell.

'*Condemned,*' hissed the echoes.

The turnkey stopped and Alfie stopped. In front of them were iron bars, reaching from floor to ceiling. An iron gate, heavily padlocked, was set into the bars. Beyond the bars was the cell.

The condemned cell was a small stone room, no bigger than cupboard. It had three walls and a stone bench that served for sitting or lying. There was no mattress, no cushions, nothing to bring any comfort. The green damp hung from the low walls and the tracks of slugs and snails glistened silver in the candlelight.

On the stone bench sat a man dressed completely in rags. His head was buried in his hands and he neither stirred nor moved his head.

In one corner of the cell was an iron candleholder which held a half-burnt candle. The draughts that whistled down the passages, and through the iron bars, blew the candle flame to one side and set the candle wax dripping down in a strangely lacy sheet. Alfie shuddered as he looked at it. A 'winding sheet' his mother used to call it and he had always hated the expression. A winding sheet for a corpse – something to wrap a dead body in.

'Going to be hanged in two days' time,' whispered the turnkey and it looked to Alfie as if the man had already, in spirit, left this world.

Alfie felt himself shivering violently. His teeth began to chatter noisily. He clenched them together, determined to show no fear, but it was too late. The turnkey had heard the clicking. He smiled maliciously. At that smile Alfie's courage came back. He straightened his back, rubbed his hands in an exaggerated way, rather like a clown pretending to be cold, and then jumped up and down, his shackles clanking noisily.

'I need a jug of hot brandy,' he said briskly and this time the turnkey laughed.

'You're a game one,' he said approvingly. 'Come on, let's get you locked up with the other chickens.'

Alfie followed the turnkey down yet another long corridor. There were a few high windows where a misty light seeped through – from the street gas lamps, he guessed. From the distance came the sound of hoarse, raucous shouts and growled deep-toned warnings. Alfie had once heard sounds like these from caged lions being wheeled in for a performance in Drury Lane Theatre.

'Animals!' The turnkey broke into his thoughts. He pointed down the corridor ahead of them. 'We found a dead man in there one morning – forty-nine men alive and one dead – and not a soul would tell us what happened during the night.'

Alfie resolved to keep his head down – terrible things could happen in Newgate jail; he had heard that.

'In here,' the turnkey said as he unlocked yet another gate and then a door beyond it.

In this huge room there was one tiny fire burning at the far end, half screened by some heavy, fearsome men with angry, belligerent faces. The fire did little good. The room was as cold as out-of-doors and somehow the fog had drifted in here and swathes of mist hovered around the heads of the prisoners.

'You take a mat down from there at night.' The

turnkey jerked a thumb at some filthy mats dangling from nails on the wall. 'That's if you can get there in time.' He gave an unpleasant laugh. 'Supper at seven,' he said and gave Alfie a little push toward a group of boys.

'Some mates of yours,' he said with a grin. 'Every one of them appeared at the Old Bailey court today – all of them condemned to hang.'

Even the oldest of the six boys looked less than fourteen. None of them took any notice of the turnkey's words; none of them seemed to be thinking about the sentence that had been passed upon them. All six were smoking old-fashioned clay pipes and they looked up from their game of cards as Alfie went by.

'Cheer up, mate!' one of them called over to Alfie with a contemptuous laugh.

'Next thing, he'll be asking for a clergyman to sob his heart out to,' sneered another.

After that, none of them bothered about Alfie and he was glad. If he were ever to get out of this place he would need everyone's good opinion and becoming friends with condemned criminals would not help. He moved away, sat down on the stone floor with his back to the wall and began to think.

He had to get out of here – before he was put on trial at the Old Bailey.

And there was only one way of getting out of here. The real murderer of Harry Booth had to be found.

But what could he do about that, locked up in prison? Alfie slumped down, his head on his knees.

The turnkey exchanged a last joke with the card-playing boys and turned to go away. As he heard their raucous laughter, Alfie sat up straight. The boys' taunts had given him an idea. He struggled to his feet and reached the turnkey before he opened the door.

'I want to see a clergyman,' he said firmly.

'Are you trying to be funny?' The turnkey stared at him with an annoyed look and the boys burst into fits of laughter again.

'He'll be the death of me,' said one, choking on his pipe.

Alfie ignored them. He kept his eyes fixed on the turnkey and his expression as bland and as polite as he could make it.

'Why didn't you say that downstairs? You was asked at the lodge did you want a clergyman and you said nuffing.' The man was furious and Alfie didn't blame him when he thought of all the long passageways and the gates and doors to be locked and unlocked.

'It was seeing the condemned man,' he said in a low voice. 'That made me feel that I wanted to say my prayers.'

And as he thought of that condemned cell, his shudder became a real one.

Would he ever sit inside those bars with only that winding sheet of candle wax to keep him company?

CHAPTER 19

THE
PRAYER

The turnkey thought for a moment and then jerked his head. 'Come on, then,' he said. 'Easier for me to take you to him, in his little room, than to bring him up here and keep him safe among all those savages. Come on, get moving and be quick about it. I haven't all day to spend with you and your fits of holiness.'

Alfie fixed his eyes on the turnkey and when the man moved, he moved with him. He got a harsh push at the door that almost knocked him down, but he staggered, then regained his balance and said nothing.

The way back was quicker. This time there was no detour to the condemned cell, just a quick march down echoing corridors, the crash of gates closing behind them, up some steps and then into the chapel.

It was a small building, just one large room with an open space and a screened-off portion to one side.

'That's where the women sit on Sundays, behind that curtain,' remarked the turnkey pointing. 'And do you see that iron cage there? Well, that's where the condemned person or persons sit the Sunday before their hanging and hear theyselves prayed for. They used to have their coffins lying beside them, but they don't do that any more – don't know why not. I used to think that it looked good. Put the frighteners on everyone, like.'

While he was speaking a white-haired, weary-looking man came in and looked surprised to see them.

'This young shaver wants to see a minister, Reverend,' said the turnkey. 'Don't mind me, covey, just talk away.'

'I think that the boy would prefer to be alone with me,' said the minister. For an old man, he had a firm, strong voice.

The turnkey shrugged his shoulders. 'Have it your own way,' he said sulkily. 'I'll be outside the door. Just remember that this varmint is going to face trial in connection with that murder at the theatre. I wouldn't trust him too far if I was you.'

'I'm sure I can come to no harm,' said the clergyman firmly. 'The boy is in chains.'

The door closed with a bit of a slam and Alfie faced the clergyman, wondering how to get around to what he wanted. He opened his mouth and then closed it again when he heard the words, 'Do you want to pray, boy?'

'Yes, sir,' said Alfie meekly. Shuffling awkwardly, he knelt down and put his hands together. He knew all about churches; he had accompanied Sammy often enough when Sammy wanted to learn a new hymn or a new Christmas carol. He saw the clergyman look at him in surprise and then a hand patted his shoulder gently. He seemed a nice old man; he must be if he chose to spend his life in a hell like Newgate prison instead of giving services in posh churches and chatting with posh ladies.

The prayer was a long one, but Alfie did not move a muscle and kept his teeth tightly clenched to avoid a yawn. His mind was working hard. Who did murder Harry Booth? He went over the information gleaned from the two clowns, Joey and Lucky. They had mentioned a few names of those who might bear a grudge. Who had the best motive? Was it John Osborne, whose face was ruined by Harry Booth? And what about Francis Fairburn, in love with Rosa, the female lead, who went off with Harry Booth? And how about the manager? Alfie could have screamed with frustration that he was not out there, investigating.

And there was more than a few shillings to be gained by solving this murder. His liberty and perhaps his life were at stake.

He would have to rely on Sarah. She was a quick-witted girl, but she did not know about Joey and Lucky, the two clowns who knew so much about Harry Booth and the other people who worked at the theatre. So this plan that he had in the back of his head just had to work.

'That's a beautiful prayer, sir,' he said opening his eyes as silence fell. 'I wish I had a copy of that to read this night before I . . . I think it would help me to sleep, sir.'

'Poor boy,' said the clergyman gently. 'Can you read?'

'And I can write,' said Alfie eagerly. 'Mr Elmore taught me – at the Ragged School of St Giles.' He could hear the turnkey clear his throat noisily a few times and then start to tramp up and down outside the door. He was getting impatient. Alfie willed the clergyman to move a bit faster.

'So you were one of his pupils,' mused the old man. 'I remember him well. He often came here to speak up for some poor lad like yourself who got into bad company. Here.' He got up and crossed the room and took a small leaf of printed paper from a cupboard, 'This is a prayer for you, my boy, you can slip that in your pocket and read it to yourself when you go back.'

'I'll have it off-by-heart in half an hour,' boasted Alfie. 'I'm very quick at learning.' He took a deep breath. 'I wish that I could send it to my sister, Sarah, then when I have learnt it.'

'Ready yet, your reverence?' called the turnkey.

'Another few minutes,' said the clergyman firmly.

'If I could just write her a few lines to go with it,' pleaded Alfie. 'You see . . . my mother asked me to look after Sarah and . . .' Inspired by the performance of the turnkey outside the door, he cleared his throat and cast down his eyes – trying to look like the picture of a brother who fears he has not set a good example to his sister.

It worked. Ignoring another question from the

turnkey, the clergyman got out a quill pen and a small jar of ink from a cupboard and set them in front of Alfie, smiling at him gently.

'I'll write on the back of the prayer,' said Alfie quickly as the clergyman wondered aloud where he had put some paper.

Rapidly he turned over the page, dipped his pen in the ink and carefully wrote:

Sister dear, when I was free,
I learnt to write, to count one, two, three.
MY PRAYER TO YOU
Find in your heart the holy three
Mary, Joseph, the babe you'll see,
You'll be lucky if that you do
And shun all clowns and actors, too.

Alfie did not take long to write the words. All through the journey down the endless, echoing passageways and while he was kneeling down, he had been perfecting his rhyme. He glanced at the clergyman, who was now kneeling in front of the altar praying. He would be unnoticed for another few minutes. He moved his paper so that the light from the gas taper fell brightly on to the page. Carefully, with the tip of his quill, Alfie put a tiny dot, almost an invisible dot, under the words *one, two, three*. Then he underlined boldly the words *clowns and actors*.

That should be enough for Sarah, he thought with satisfaction. Sarah had brains. She would understand to look at the number one word on the first line – *find*; the number two word on the second line, *Joseph*; and the third word on the third line, *lucky*. The message would be clear: *Find Joseph, Lucky, clowns and actors*. Hopefully the two clowns would repeat the gossip about the actors, Francis Fairburn and John Osborne. Tomorrow, he remembered, was her half-day holiday so surely she and the rest of the gang would visit him. There definitely could be no objection to him handing her a prayer.

'I've finished, sir,' he said softly, just as a loud rap and the words, 'You all right in there, your reverence?' sounded from the door.

'Perfectly all right, officer,' said the clergyman in a slightly impatient voice.

'Would you read what I said, sir?' pleaded Alfie. 'Will I be able to give that to my sister if she visits me?'

'Well!' The man was a fast reader. He scanned the page, put it down and looked searchingly at Alfie. He seemed surprised by the words so Alfie hastened to explain.

'She wants to go on the stage, my sister, sir. I want

to try to stop her. You know what happens to girls who go on the stage. My mother would never have let her do that.'

'Quite right, too! Well, Mr Elmore used to tell me that he had some very bright, clever pupils and I can see that you must be one of them. That's a clever piece of verse. I'm sure your sister will take that to heart.'

'Mr Elmore used to say that people remember things better if they are in verse,' murmured Alfie, hoping that he hadn't been too clever for his own good. The man had picked up the page again and his eyes seemed glued to the words.

'Quite right, quite right! And did he teach you some of the beautiful psalms?' To Alfie's great relief he moved his eyes from the paper and looked at Alfie with a smile.

'Yes, sir. I think I had better go now, sir, the warder is getting impatient. I'd like to come again, sir, some time, if I could . . .'

'The boy would like to come again some time, officer,' said the clergyman, opening the door. He still kept the paper in his hand. 'I've given him this prayer so that he may read it to himself and if his sister visits tomorrow he wants to give it to her. Will that be all right?' He moved the prayer slightly as the turnkey seemed about to snatch it from him.

Quite a courageous old cove, thought Alfie, making sure to keep his face bland and innocent. He, himself, could not afford to annoy the turnkey in any way.

'Not up to me what he gives to the sister – that will be up to them in the lodge, but he can keep that with him if wants to,' said the turnkey. He gazed with such a blank face at the prayer that Alfie immediately suspected that the man could not read. His spirits rose. A warder might have been more suspicious of his strange poem than an innocent old clergyman.

'Thank you, sir,' said Alfie with relief. He made a respectful bow to the clergyman, muttered his thanks again and clanked his way down the stone passageway feeling a little more hopeful. Was it possible that he had taken the first step towards freeing himself from the most dreaded, most fearful prison in the world?

CHAPTER 20

THE MISSING FINGER

'Tom,' said Sammy.

'What?' asked Tom in a bad-tempered manner. He chewed on the remains of the crust from the loaf that Sarah had brought yesterday. He was in a furious mood. He was annoyed with himself and that made things worse. Jack had asked him to go down to the river, but he had refused irritably.

Why had he allowed himself to sick up that pie? It was the best piece of food that he had seen for a month. He felt really hungry this morning and the bread wasn't helping much.

That was not the worst thing, though.

Why had he been tricked into telling Sarah that he was the one who betrayed Alfie? He'd never hear the end of it, he thought gloomily. Even Jack was hardly speaking to him this morning. Jack, unusually for him, had even gone so far as to say firmly that neither he, Sammy nor Sarah would have told.

He had been fool enough to tell that cove about Alfie, Tom told himself savagely, but he was even more of a fool to let it out to Sarah. There was no need. After all, the man could have found that bit of information from lots of people – Betty for instance.

'You know that fellow who got you to tell him about Alfie,' began Sammy.

'Oh, shut up,' said Tom viciously. 'Shut up or I'll hit you; blind or not, you'll feel the weight of my fist.'

'I was thinking that we could put our ideas together,' said Sammy mildly. He took very little notice of Tom. Tom was always all bark and no bite. In any case, Mutsy would never allow him to hurt Sammy. Mutsy was lying very close to Sammy this morning, bewildered by the absence of Alfie. Never before had a whole night gone by without Alfie appearing and somehow the big dog knew that. Sammy stroked him gently and felt the dog nuzzle up to him.

'What ideas?' Tom sounded more sullen than angry now.

'Well, I was wondering if you noticed anything funny about this geezer – anything about his hands?'

'His hands? Nah, I didn't notice nothing – he had gloves on.'

'Yeah, leather ones.' Sammy thought hard. 'What did the gloves look like?'

'Couldn't tell you. I didn't take no notice.' Tom was getting bored.

'Did he take them off when he handed you the pie?'

'What do you want to know that for?' Tom sounded suspicious, as if he felt that Sammy was trying to trap him into something.

'Just wondered.'

'You can stop talking about the pie. I'm sick of the pie. It's all right for you. People look at you and say, "Oh, that poor itty blind boy, let's give him something to eat". They don't do that to me. There you were, stuffing your face with chestnuts, and me so hungry that I thought I would faint if I didn't get food. How was I to know that Alfie would be fool enough to hang around the theatre for the whole day? I'd have thought he'd have found a good hiding place as soon as he got in there, and stayed put.'

Sammy ignored this. 'It's just that I keep thinking about the hand on my arm. There was something funny about it.'

'What was funny?' Tom began to sound interested. 'He was wearing a glove, you said so yourself.'

Sammy nodded. 'Yes, I could feel it and I could smell it, as well. But I don't think it was a thick glove . . .'

'You're right,' Tom broke in excitedly. 'You're right, Sammy. Is that giving you an idea? He was wearing gloves all the time, fancy ones – sort of yellow leather – very fancy, with stitching on them. I'd say they would be thin gloves, too.'

'So that he wouldn't need to take them off in the ordinary way,' said Sammy.

'Let me think. Yeah, you're right. He didn't take them off when he . . .'

'Handed you the pie,' said Sammy in a matter-of-fact way. 'Are you sure? Think hard, Tom. We're doing great, the two of us. Think hard. Get a picture of them in your mind.'

Tom shut his eyes. It was funny, he thought, how that helped you to remember things. Everyone remarked on how smart Sammy was, but when he closed his eyes he, also, had a feeling of being clever. Perhaps being blind sharpened your wits.

'Two hands, or one, on the plate?' came Sammy's voice.

'Two,' said Tom, still keeping his eyes tightly screwed up. He knew what Sammy was at – trying to get him to remember the scene as clearly as possible. 'Two,' he repeated, 'and – I'm certain now – the gloves were on his hands, definitely.'

Sammy smiled with satisfaction. It was not proof, but at the same time the very fact that this mysterious man had kept on his gloves, had risked the valuable yellow leather being stained by a splash of gravy – this seemed to back up his own memory. He held out his own hands, trying to visualise how a metal plate would be carried.

'Thumbs on top and fingers underneath,' said Tom. 'Definitely gloves!'

'You know the way, when someone grabs your arm, that you feel the fingers?' Sammy reached out, his hand fumbling until it met Tom's arm and then gripped it tightly.

'You're right – I do feel your fingers. Every single one of them.'

'And now?'

'You've bent one of them back; I can only feel three!' cried Tom.

'That's it! That's what I felt! The man was missing a finger from his right hand!'

'Is that a clue?' Tom sounded hopeful.

'I think it could be. It's a reason to keep his gloves on, anyway. That missing finger could give him away,' said Sammy. 'Now we have something to tell Alfie. But how are we going to do it?'

CHAPTER 21

NEWGATE RATS

Alfie thought it was the longest night of his life. There were only enough mats for about half the prisoners and Alfie didn't even try to get one. He just stayed where he was, sitting on the cold bare stone floor, his knees hunched up, his shackled ankles sore from the weight of the iron. He put his head into his hands and tried to sleep, but the cold iron of the manacles kept waking him up. The fire began to die down and the moon shone through a tiny window high on the wall. By its light, Alfie could see a large rat emerge from its hole and scuttle along the side of the crumbling wall. It sniffed at the pocket of one of the prisoners who yelled and lashed out with his shackled foot and the frightened rat scaled Alfie's legs and returned to his hole in the wall.

After that Alfie dared not sleep. He stayed awake watching the lice crawl across the stone floor, their hard, shiny backs glinting in the moonlight. What time was it, he wondered. He hoped that half of the night was over, but he guessed from the height of the moon that it was probably only about midnight.

And then he heard a bell ring. It seemed to come from under the flagstones. He started violently. He wasn't the only one. Everyone woke up and listened.

'It's the bellman from the Old Bailey church,' said an elderly man to Alfie. 'They ring one minute after midnight for the condemned man.'

'Just to give him a good night's sleep,' said one of the boys and all the others laughed.

One of the boys began to chant in a loud, cheerful voice as if the whole thing was just a joke:

'*All you that in the condemned hold do lie,*
Prepare you, for tomorrow you shall die;
Watch all and pray, the hour is drawing near
That you before the Almighty must appear;
Examine well yourselves, in time repent
That you may not to eternal flames be sent:
And when St Sepulchre's bell tomorrow tolls

The Lord above have mercy on your souls
Past twelve o'clock!'

'There will be another poor soul tomorrow,' said the elderly man to Alfie with a sigh. 'You get used to the nightly lullaby in this place.'

'Visitors for our Holy Joe here,' said the turnkey with a sneer. He jerked his head at Alfie.

Alfie got quietly to his feet, feeling his pocket to make sure that the piece of paper with the prayer was still there safely. At noon he had slept for a few hours and now he was stiff from lying, shackled and handcuffed, on the bare stones of the floor. It was all beginning to seem like a bad dream to him.

But now, at the turnkey's words, every fibre within him was quivering and ready for action.

He followed the line of men who had been summoned. No one had come to visit the boys and they seemed a bit glum about that, calling out jeers and swear words after him.

'Is it my sister?' he asked the turnkey as the key was being turned in the lock.

'How do I know? I just obey orders.' He was extra bad-tempered with Alfie. Probably he sensed that, in some way, Alfie had hoodwinked him during that long session in the church with the chaplain.

The turnkey stopped when they reached the felons' quadrangle, where Alfie and the other prisoners, all heavily shackled and manacled, had dragged their legs around for half an hour that morning. 'Stand!' he roared and lashed out with his truncheon at one old man who had not stopped quickly enough to suit him.

'Wait,' he yelled again and then two other warders came out of the lodge, swishing heavy truncheons to warn the prisoners not to bolt.

It would have been useless to try anything. They were in a concrete yard with twenty-foot high walls around the four sides of it. They waited, shivering in the rain. There seemed to be something going on in the building on the right-hand side – a clanking of iron bars, creaking sounds and hammering. The wait was long and dreary. The rain was heavy and the prisoners' rough clothing soaked up the wet.

'Have to search the visitors, lads; that takes time,' said one of the warders eventually.

And then there was another wait. Alfie thought he would scream if it were any longer. He began to worry about the prayer in his pocket. Would they search the prisoners as well as the visitors? Perhaps he should mention the prayer first before it was found on him. These two warders did not look too bad.

One had almost a pleasant face, and Alfie approached him, moving slowly and watching his reactions carefully. He raised his right arm as he had been taught to do in school and the movement brought a reluctant grin to the man's face.

'What's the problem, young shaver?' he asked.

'Please, sir,' said Alfie with extreme politeness. 'The turnkey said that it would be all right to give this to my sister. He said to tell you that it came from the chaplain in the prison church, sir,' he lied with a sudden happy inspiration. They seemed to think a lot of religion in this prison so that might work.

The warder gave the prayer a keen glance, but did not bother turning it over. 'All right,' he said. 'I'll pass it over.'

Why can't I give it myself? wondered Alfie. He was disappointed, as he had meant to give Sarah some sort of signal as he handed it over that this piece of paper was of significance. He just had to trust that Sarah would really get the paper – and realise what it meant.

However, when they went into the visiting room, he could see why it had been taken from him.

It was a fair-sized room, but it had been divided

into three sections by bars, only six inches apart and stretching from floor to ceiling.

The prisoners, with their warders, were at the nearest side of the room and the visitors, with two more truncheon-bearing warders, were at the far end.

And the middle – a space of about six feet – was completely empty, barred off from prisoners and visitors.

No visitor, no prisoner, could hand anything, whether it was a tasty cake or a weapon, across that space.

There were plenty of visitors that day. An old woman in rags, a few warmly dressed men who seemed very uneasy in the prison surroundings, women with children clutching to them, most with a baby in their arms, a few others who were well known to the warders and engaged in jokes and banter with them. And then there were Sarah and the three boys. Sarah held Sammy's hand and Jack had his arm around Tom's shoulders. Tom's face looked white through the grime, but Sammy was his usual calm self. They had not brought Mutsy – that was probably sensible, but Alfie got a lump in his throat as he wondered whether he would ever see his poor old faithful dog again.

One by one the prisoners were called to come up,

to stand like wild tigers peering through the bars. None of the visitors stayed long, Alfie noticed. It was very difficult to talk across that empty space and especially to talk with all the listening ears. He had imagined that they would be private.

And now it was his turn. He moved to the bars and stood there. For the first time since he was a baby he could not think of anything to say. He just stared at them. It occurred to him that he was now completely powerless – he, Alfie, who always managed to find a solution. His belief in himself had ebbed away.

'Alfie, I got your prayer.' Sarah's voice was calm and matter-of-fact and carried well across the space. Alfie was very thankful about that – thankful for her casual, collected manner. 'You needn't worry about us, Alfie,' she went on. 'We've got everything under control. I hope a gentleman that we know will be able to help you.'

What did she mean, wondered Alfie. Did she mean that she had found the murderer? Could that be possible? But she couldn't have. She didn't know enough. None of them knew enough. More work needed to be done, more investigation. Still, he felt consoled. She had got the paper and she had brains, he told himself.

'Would you like Sammy to sing you a song, Alfie?' asked Sarah and without waiting for a reply she turned to the warder. 'Would that be all right, sir, if the blind boy sings?'

There was a moment's silence. One warder looked at the other and then they looked across at the warders in the opposite cage.

'Sing?' said one in a dubious tone of voice.

'I don't suppose there can be anything agin it.'

'Might be against regulations.'

'They can talk, can't they? No difference, ain't there?'

'That's right,' agreed the other reluctantly. 'T'ain't no difference. Go ahead, sonny, sing your brother a lullaby.'

Then he whispered something and the other warder roared with laughter – something about hanging, probably, thought Alfie. Warders seemed to find that a great joke.

And then Sammy began to sing. He sang a song about a woman stitching a shirt. It was always a great favourite with the well-dressed lady shoppers in Covent Garden: they seemed to love songs about poor people!

There was another joke from one of the warders

and a roar of laughter, echoed immediately by the visitors and those prisoners who looked for favour. The audience had got bored with the singing and had stopped listening.

And then Sammy began to sing the chorus and only Alfie, who had heard his brother sing that song hundreds of times, realised that Sammy, instead of singing the chorus: *stitch, stitch, stitch*, had substituted the words *fingers, fingers, fingers*.

Another joke from the comedian warder, another roar of laughter and Sammy went on fearlessly, his high voice penetrating through the shouts of laughter and the filthy jokes to reach his brother on the other side of the divided room.

'Only three fingers, only three fingers
Three fingers on the hand,
We saw three fingers alone,
Yellow gloves on the hand,
One big finger was gone.'

And then Sammy sang the rest of the verses of the famous melody 'Song of the Shirt', his face serious.

When the song ended, he stopped and waited unselfconsciously. This was always the moment when the applause came, and after a minute one of the warders said, 'Very nice, lad – now number thirteen.'

And number thirteen came forward to listen to his aged mother complaining about his conduct and asking him how he expected her to live without anyone to support her.

Sarah bobbed politely to the warders and led the boys from the room without even a backward glance. But she left Alfie's mind buzzing.

Three fingers! We saw three fingers alone, Sammy had sung. It made him think of . . . What was it?

It could be a vital clue, if only he could remember!

But it would be another week before he could have visitors again.

Would he still be alive by next Monday?

CHAPTER 22

FRUSTRATION

Alfie racked his brains as he followed the turnkey down the long passageways, and through all of the locked gates. What was that picture that kept flitting into his mind and then oozing away again? What could it be? Something about fingers . . .

It was only when he was back in the prison room that suddenly he remembered.

Harry Booth, there in front of the curtains. The intensely white limelight. Alfie clenched his hands and willed the vision to become clearer. Yes! Harry Booth had walked on stage. The riot began. The noise, the smell, the sights of that night at Covent Garden

Theatre came back to Alfie. Harry Booth there, yelling at the top of his voice but no one listening. The curtains parting – just a crack. The hand coming out, coming from behind the gap between the two curtains. A frilly sleeve, edged with a thin fringe of orange fur – the colour of Joey's wig ... A clown's sleeve. The hand moved down. It was pouring now. Pouring something from the glass phial. Something strange about that hand.

It had bothered him all of the days since and suddenly now his memory was clear and pin-sharp.

The hand that poured that deadly dose into Harry Booth's port had been missing a finger.

What was it that Sammy had sung? '*We saw three fingers alone.*'

Alfie put his head in his hands and thought hard.

Who was the man with a missing finger?

Did he have anything to do with John Osborne, or Francis Fairburn, or even the manager?

'*Yellow gloves,*' Sammy had sung. Alfie kept his hands over his eyes. He could not afford to allow anything to distract him at this vital moment. His mind was clear and working fast and at once he knew where he had seen yellow gloves. The picture was very clear in Alfie's mind. Himself and Mutsy, juggling, turning cartwheels, dancing – desperately doing anything that would attract the attention of the rich people who only wanted to get indoors out of the freezing fog . . .

And the man that stopped. The small, fat man with his hat pulled down over his face. The man that praised his performance – this man was wearing yellow gloves as he pulled out a bunch of tickets from his pocket.

Why wear gloves when you are handling something as thin as paper tickets?

Unless, of course, that you have something to hide – like a missing finger!

But why start a riot? Why hand out tickets for a performance where you have planned a murder?

It just didn't make sense.

Did something happen that made the man in yellow gloves decide to murder Harry Booth?

What was it that the clown had said about Harry Booth?

'Always had his nose in other people's business; that was Harry Booth for you.'

Alfie sprang to his feet and gazed desperately around the crowded room, eyeing the couple of small windows high up in the wall and the locked door. He clenched his fists. Frustration was boiling within him. He felt like screaming, or kicking the door, or trying to scale the chimney above the tiny, smoking fire.

He needed to be out there, snooping around, asking questions, finding out if his suspicions were correct, with the help of his gang, not stuck in here, waiting to be hanged!

CHAPTER 23

THE
PUZZLE

'What are they doing?' asked Tom fearfully. He, Jack, Sammy and Sarah had just come out of the prison and had been stopped by a guard at the gate. Stout boards, painted black were being placed around the entrance to Newgate and in front of the yard beside it.

'Getting ready for a hanging,' said the warder cheerfully. 'They have to keep the crowd back. Tomorrow morning they'll stop the traffic until it's all over. It's a great sight. People pay any money to rent one of the windows around here so that they can look down and see everything. The more hangings there are, the more money is made. Listen! Hear that hammering. They're starting to put the gallows together. Look over there in the yard. Can you see they're building a platform outside that door? What's the matter with the boy?'

'He's sick,' said Sarah. She stood still for a moment, holding tightly to Sammy's arm. Jack had gone after Tom who was vomiting into the gutter.

'A relation of yours? The man for the high drop tomorrow?' enquired the warder. 'Sorry if I upset your brother.'

'No, no relation of ours,' said Sarah calmly. 'Tom's eaten something that disagreed with him.'

'Greedy, eh?' The warder laughed. 'You can go now; you'll get through over there. That fellow will let you past the barrier.'

'You all right, Tom?' asked Sammy as Jack and Tom joined them.

'Yeah,' said Tom. 'Get off.' He shook his brother's arm from his shoulder. 'I'm going back,' he said. 'Mutsy's been on his own for long enough.' He set off at a run, dodging in and out of the crowd that was flocking to Newgate to see the spectacle of the gallows being raised.

'Leave him.' Sarah grabbed Jack's wrist. 'He'll be better on his own.'

'He probably wants to be alone with Mutsy,' said Sammy. There was a slightly bleak note in his voice, and Sarah, looking at him, wondered how often things got so bad for Sammy that only the presence of a warmly loving dog could comfort him.

'We'll walk slowly then and give him some time,' she decided. 'At least we'll have something to eat when we get back. The cook's good; she always gives me a basket of left-overs on my half holiday. I tell her that I am going to visit my Aunt Minnie who is bedridden. I'm beginning to believe in Aunt Minnie and her faithful dog myself.'

There was no response from either of the boys so she went on. 'I tell the cook so many stories about Mutsy that now she always gives me a bone for him. Let's hope that she never decides to accompany me to see the poor lady.' She tried to laugh but Jack didn't respond and Sammy turned his head alertly in her direction as though he sensed something that was not in her light-hearted words. He said nothing, though, and the three walked in silence down Fleet Street until they passed under Temple Bar.

'What are we going to do?' asked Jack despairingly as they turned up towards Drury Lane. 'I just keep thinking that we should be doing something. Should I

154

go and see Inspector Denham? He knows Alfie. He'd know that Alfie could have had nothing to do with the murder on the stage.'

Sarah thought about that for a minute. Alfie was waiting for his trial, but he was being treated like a criminal. Inspector Denham was the chief policeman at Bow Street Police Station – and yes, he did know Alfie, had used him on occasions in his investigations, but would he interfere in Scotland Yard business? Sarah thought not. And perhaps he might be annoyed that they came to him when it was not a Bow Street Police Station matter. On the other hand, Inspector Denham could probably tell them when Alfie would be tried. What would be the best thing to do? If Alfie were here, he would tell them, but now it was up to her. Jack was a nice fellow, but he was a follower, not a leader.

'Leave it for the moment,' she decided. 'It would be better to go to Inspector Denham when we have something to report. Some sort of suspicion. We have no real evidence yet.' She thought again about the glass phial with the greasy finger marks picked out by the dust. She clicked her tongue in exasperation at the idiocy of that Officer Grey from Scotland Yard shoving it into his pocket where the rough wool would rub it clean after an hour or so.

* * *

The fire was bright when they got back to the cellar and Tom was looking a little less white. Perhaps ten minutes alone with Mutsy had done him good. The big dog came over, tail wagging, sniffed each one of them carefully, looked at the door and then sank down, with a sigh, at Sammy's feet. Alfie had never been absent from Mutsy for as long as this since Mutsy had joined the gang in the Bow Street cellar. Sarah stroked the side of his face and he gave a subdued flip of his tail, but his eyes were fixed mournfully on the door and he did not even sit up when Sarah opened her basket and took out a juicy bone wrapped in brown paper. She put it down in front of him and he just lay there gazing at it for a minute before beginning to crunch it. Sarah blinked hard and returned to her basket.

'Plenty for everyone,' she said, trying to sound cheerful. No one responded so she dug into her pocket and produced a twopenny piece – change from the sixpence given to her by Officer Grey.

'See if you can get some small beer with that, Jack,' she said. 'Tom, get out the mugs.'

Beer would liven up the boys, she hoped, and when Jack came back with a jugful, she made sure that Tom had a good share of it.

'What about the prayer thing that Alfie gave you?' asked Jack.

'He must've given up,' said Tom hoarsely. 'I never thought I'd see the day when Alfie would start saying prayers.' He crashed his pewter mug on the table and dropped to his knees, burying his head in Mutsy's fur. 'I wish . . . I just wish I'd never done it,' he said brokenly. 'I were that . . . I were that hungry! I just didn't know what I was doing, sort of. I were out of my head with hunger. The words just came out . . . I wish I were dead . . . I do . . .'

'Alfie hasn't given up, Tom, no way. That prayer – that's just a trick, ain't it, Sarah?' cried Jack. 'Come on, Tom. Have a sup of beer and you'll feel better.'

'He's right, Tom,' said Sarah. 'I bet it's just a trick. We'll have something to eat and then we'll all put our heads together.' She addressed the words to Tom, but looked at Sammy. She could see how intently the blind boy listened and how his clenched hand opened and relaxed.

'Let's look at it, then,' said Tom, raising his head. He drank a little beer and then pushed it away.

'Eat first,' said Sarah firmly. She waited until the last crumb had gone, before she looked down once more at the prayer that she held in her hand. 'Look, you can see, Jack, you can see that Alfie has underlined the words *clowns and actors* so he must want me to talk to one of the clowns or one of the actors. I know the two actors that he was talking about. But which of the clowns?'

'Read it out, will you, Sarah?' asked Tom humbly. He still felt sick. The sight of Alfie in that terrible place would never leave him, he thought miserably. He tried to tell himself that Alfie might have got caught in any case, but somehow he didn't believe it. Alfie always pulled off anything that he attempted. The one thing that Alfie would never have thought of was that he would be betrayed by one of his own gang.

Tom listened attentively to Alfie's message – yes it was definitely about clowns and actors, but, as Sarah asked, which ones?

'Can I look at it?' Tom asked. He had very good eyes; Alfie had often said that. Perhaps there might be something that Sarah hadn't noticed. He held the piece of paper to the light of the fire and screwed up his eyes. 'Light the candle, will you, Jack?' He said the words without removing his eyes from the page.

Jack obediently lit a candle. They didn't often bother with one – candles cost money – but this was an emergency.

'I see something now,' said Tom excitedly. The candle cast a great light on the page, a white light. 'Did you see, Sarah? He's put little dots under some of the words. Read it out again. Slowly this time! Point to each word as you read it and I'll show you where the dots are.'

So, slowly and carefully, like a learner reading the first primer, Sarah read, with Tom's head looking over her shoulder, his eyes following each word that she pointed to.

'Sister dear, when I was free,
I learnt to write, to count one, two, three.'

'There,' shouted Tom. 'Look there's dots under *one, two, three.'*

'MY PRAYER TO YOU,' continued Sarah,
Find in your heart the holy three
Mary, Joseph, the babe you'll see,
You'll be lucky if that you do
And shun all clowns and actors, too.'

'Why did he talk about learning to count up to three?' mused Sammy. 'Don't suppose he learnt that at school. He could always do that.'

'I bet I know why he put that *one, two, three!'* Sarah sounded excited. 'It's a clue. You have to pick out the first word on line one, the second word on line two and the third word on line three.'

'What are they, Sarah?' Tom was almost bursting with impatience. 'Go on, read them out!'

'Wait.' Sarah ran her finger along the lines. '*Find . . . Joseph . . . Lucky.* That's the message.'

'Lucky is the sort of name that a clown would have,' chimed in Sammy.

'*Joey the Clown*, I've seen that sign outside a booth – you know like one of the Punch and Judy things but full length in Clare Market,' said Jack. 'He had a couple of those Chinese lanterns – pretty they were.'

'That's the message then,' said Sarah. 'Find those two clowns – they might be able to give us the information we need. We just want to know if one of the other clowns has a missing first finger. Or perhaps it is one of them – either Joey or Lucky. Anyway, a missing finger should be noticeable to anyone who worked with him.'

'I'll do it,' said Tom. 'I'll go down to the theatre at Covent Garden tomorrow. I'll ask for some work, hang around a bit . . .'

'That's right,' said Sarah. 'Take care, though – don't stick your nose out too far. And always make sure that there's an open door so that you can run if necessary.'

She would have preferred to question the clowns herself – to question them in a way that did not arouse their suspicions. But what could she do? She dare not show her nose inside that theatre again and she would lose her job if she took time off tomorrow.

And time, for Alfie, might be running out.

CHAPTER 24

A FIGHT
AGAINST TIME

'It's up to us now,' said Jack solemnly as he carefully divided the remaining hunk of bread into three equal pieces, placing one in front of Tom and guiding Sammy's hand towards the other one.

'That's right,' agreed Sammy. He chewed his bread carefully and then said, 'We all need to work. Tom is going to the theatre. That'll be the most important thing, but I think I'll go and have a chat with Inspector Denham.'

'Sarah said not yet,' said Tom.

'Sarah don't know everything,' responded Sammy tranquilly. 'I'm Alfie's brother and it makes sense that

I'd be worried about him. Inspector Denham won't mind me coming. Anyway, being blind and all that, the constables won't want to turn me out – like they might with either you or Jack. If Jack walks with me to the outside of the place, Mutsy will look after me then. Not a bad idea to teach the old fellow the word *police*, anyway,' he added. 'Never know when I'd want that.'

'What shall I do?' To Sammy's sensitive ear, Jack's voice sounded strained and unhappy.

'Why don't you go to Scotland Yard? Ask for that Officer Grey. You might get thrown out on your ear, but then again, you mightn't. Act like Alfie. Say you've information of great importance about the Covent Garden murder. Can't do any harm. Talk to him. Tell him what Sarah was telling us – about the other men who might want Harry Booth dead. Them clowns mightn't want to mention that to a policeman – they say that actors always stick together and the same would be for clowns – so the chances are that he knows nothing about it.'

'I'd just like to see Inspector Denham for a few minutes.'

It was a nuisance, thought Sammy, that he couldn't see the face in front of him. He didn't know whether the constable was on the point of saying yes or saying no. He could sense his embarrassment though, so he waited peacefully and hoped for the best.

'What about the dog?' asked another voice, well lowered, but certainly easily heard by anyone with normal hearing.

'He can't walk without him,' replied the constable in the same tone of voice.

Thinks I'm deaf as well as blind, and crippled, too, Sammy thought, and suppressed a grin. It didn't matter to him what they said, or thought, as long as one of them brought him into Inspector Denham.

'Wait a minute, sonny. I'll . . .' Then there was a sound of a door opening and straightaway Inspector's Denham's voice.

'You're young Alfie's brother, aren't you? Come in. Go on, bring the dog too. That's the dog that rescued you a while back, isn't it? Clever fellow! Alfie told me all about it. Constable, put that chair there so that the lad can sit down – Sammy, isn't it?'

'That's right, sir,' said Sammy putting his hand behind him to find the chair and then lowering himself into it. Mutsy's warm bulk was beside him and he kept his hand on the dog's neck and hoped that things would go well.

'Alfie's in prison – in Newgate.' He let the statement

hang for a minute. He could feel the sympathy in the air, could sense the small, uneasy movements.

'I just heard that this morning. I was away yesterday. I was very sorry, indeed, to hear the news. I'm afraid that it has nothing to do with me. It's in the hands of Scotland Yard . . .'

For a moment Sammy thought Inspector Denham was going to say something else, but after the silence had lasted a good ten seconds he said, 'Thank you, sir,' and waited. There was more to come, he knew.

And then the door shut. The inspector must have nodded to the constable to go out and to leave them alone. When he spoke next, his voice sounded different, less official, more friendly . . .

'Your brother can call on someone to be a witness as to good character, Sammy,' he said gently. 'I will be happy to do this. I'll send a note to the prison. I can certainly bear witness to his hard work at school and how quickly he learnt to read and write and . . . and . . . well, I can mention that he has assisted the police once or twice . . . not make too much of it, you understand. That might give him a reputation of being a police spy, or something like that – last thing that Alfie would want. Anyway, I'll be there and I'll do my best for him. Don't worry.'

'Thank you, sir,' repeated Sammy. 'I just wanted to ask you a question. Why is he in prison? Why have the Scotland Yard men arrested him? Alfie didn't do nothing.'

'They think that he is part of a gang,' explained the inspector. 'Gangs are using children more and more these days. They send them through windows too small for grown men – to open the front door to the thieves – and they use them for pickpocketing, and to distract attention from their crimes. Apparently Alfie came on the stage, through a trapdoor, and the police think that the poison was slipped into the glass of port while Harry Booth and the audience were all looking at Alfie, popping up on stage like a jack-in-the-box.'

'I see,' said Sammy. 'But Alfie just came on to the stage because he saw someone put the poison into the port. He tried to stop Harry Booth drinking it but he was too late.'

'It's a possible story.' Inspector Denham sounded dubious. 'It just depends on what the judge thinks about it. And the jury, of course. There'll be a jury of twelve men when his case comes on. It all depends . . .'

The awkwardness in his voice was easy to hear, thought Sammy. Things were bad for Alfie. The Scotland Yard people thought that if he were put in prison he would come out with the name of the gang, or the gang leader, and then when he didn't they would be happy enough to see him take the whole blame. And the crime was murder . . .

'Could you tell me, sir, when the trial will come on?' He asked the question as steadily and calmly as he could, but was not able to stop himself starting when Inspector Denham said, his voice heavy with sympathy, 'I'm afraid it will be held on Friday.'

Friday! Sammy felt as if his heart had stopped.

Today was Tuesday.

Only three more days, and a sentence of death might be passed on his brother.

CHAPTER 25

DISAPPOINTMENT

Tom was in luck. The man at the desk offered him two pence to pick up the rotten oranges, putrid old potatoes and the squashed tomatoes from the floors before the cleaners started work.

'Trouble again last night?' queried Tom, accepting a cluster of buckets and picking up the broom in his other hand.

'Worse than ever! Hardly anyone in the posh seats – no one wants to pay good money just to see a riot! It's no good. You can't run a theatre like this on the prices of the cheapest seats. Lots of the rioters probably had faked tickets anyway, just like before,' said the man. 'Off you go, and do it quietly. The clowns are having their rehearsal in a few minutes so keep away from the stage.'

Tom worked hard and fast, scouring the ground between the seats, under the seats and in the aisles. There was plenty to pick up. He filled three buckets and was about to go back to the desk to get some more when suddenly a man came along and lit the limelights at the foot of the stage.

Suddenly a pair of clowns ran on to the stage, screaming with laughter, poking each other, telling jokes and turning cartwheels. Tom was so fascinated that he had to remind himself to carry on picking up the rubbish that the rioters had hurled around the theatre the night before.

And then came another couple; these weren't so good – they just threw water over each other and hurled custard pies, which the other always caught to prevent a mess. They were followed by a pair of clowns with a small dog wearing a bridle, reins and harness, just like a horse, and pulling a tiny carriage behind him. Tom took careful note of this as it was a trick that they could easily teach Mutsy. Jack was clever with his hands and always on the look-out for things thrown on rubbish heaps. A couple of wheels and a lightweight box made from some pieces of old timber – that would make a showy sight with Mutsy pulling it, thought Tom.

But then everything went out of his head. The next two clowns were exchanging insults, calling taunts across the stage to each other.

And the names that they were shouting were Joey and Lucky.

Instantly Tom went into action. He picked up a few more tomatoes and oranges, gathered up his full bucket and went back out to the man at the desk.

'Done that,' he said cheerily. 'All right if I go back stage? Saw an orange or two sticking out from under the curtain.'

The man barely nodded. He was busy sorting out the torn ticket halves, putting some aside and throwing the others in the bin.

Tom seized an empty bucket, transferred a few oranges into it while the man was not looking and moved off fast. He would try to be backstage before the clowns arrived.

'That was a great act,' he said breathlessly when they came off. He looked narrowly at their hands. Lucky was easing off an uncomfortable shoe and Joey was taking off his wig and clown's pointed hat. Both of them had all of their fingers.

Sammy was standing there in Covent Garden market, singing, when Tom came out of the theatre. The rain had stopped. It was foggy, but not as bad as some of the other days so there were a few people around. Tom stood and watched while some people threw halfpence into Sammy's cap.

I'll wait until he finishes the next song, he told himself but he knew that he wanted to put off the moment when he had to break the truth to Sammy.

According to Joey and Lucky, there weren't any clowns with missing fingers.

'Any luck?' Tom asked, as Jack arrived at Covent Garden market shortly afterwards.

'Nah,' said his brother shortly. 'They wouldn't let me go near the place. Said that Officer Grey was busy, that he was out on a case. Told me to get out and not to show my face again.'

'Well, Sammy has a bit of good news,' said Tom, trying to be cheerful. 'Tell him what Inspector Denham said, Sam.'

'You tell him,' said Sammy, fumbling on the ground for his cap. He sorted out the coins – counted them – threepence, took out the sixpenny coin that Inspector

Denham had given him and handed the whole ninepence to Jack. Jack was now in charge of the little gang. It looked like there was going to be no easy way out of Newgate for Alfie.

Sammy put on his cap and said, 'Home, Mutsy,' as bravely as he could.

As they made their way back to the cellar, Sammy could hear Tom telling Jack how Inspector Denham was going to speak up for Alfie. But Sammy did not share his cousin's belief in Inspector Denham. Tom had not heard the tone of the man's voice, but he had.

And there wasn't much comfort in it.

CHAPTER 26

UNRAVELLING

The shout came just as they reached the top of the steps. Jack had gone off to buy supper so only Sammy and Tom were there. This time the sound was unmistakable and they both turned and waited.

'Tom!' yelled a voice.

'Someone calling you.' Sammy went on down the steps. He felt terribly weary, almost as though his legs would no longer carry him. As far back as he could remember Alfie was always the one that he turned to when he needed help. And now Alfie needed his help and he had none to give him. This murder had to be solved and to be solved quickly. He turned the key in the lock and went in, leaving the door open for Tom. There was little warmth coming from the fire – they were short of coal – but Sammy felt his way over and sat as near to it as possible. He buried his head in his hands, conscious that Mutsy was leaning up against him.

He was roused by a harsh bark. There was a sudden rushing of air, a scrabbling of nails on the floor, and then the bark came again – loud and aggressive.

'Great balls of fire!' exclaimed a strange voice.

'Mutsy! Down!' yelled Tom.

'Mutsy, here, boy.' Sammy clicked his fingers and Mutsy returned to him.

'Codlins and Short!' said another voice, in a high-pitched tone. 'I thought my last hour had come, Joey! Is that a dog, or just a small donkey?'

'Are you a clown or a mouse, Lucky?' asked the first voice, also in that strange, high-pitched tone.

Sammy heard Tom laugh and knew that all was well. 'Say you're sorry, Mutsy,' he said cheerfully and listened with pleasure to the high-pitched laugh – a clown's laugh. He had heard them often enough at the markets and Alfie had often described their routine. He knew why they were laughing now – Mutsy would be going through one of his routines where he sat on his back legs and hid his eyes behind his paws.

'That's no donkey, dunderhead!' said one. 'That's a clown. Why isn't he on the stage? That's what I say, Joey.'

'He can do hundreds of tricks,' boasted Tom.

'And who's this young gentleman?'

'I'm Sammy.'

'I'm Joey the clown,' Sammy felt his hand taken in a friendly squeeze, 'and this is my partner, Lucky. So you live here by yourselves – four boys, no mother or father, is that right?' He sounded sorry for them.

'That's right. Do you know Alfie?' Jack had arrived back in time to answer the last question. Sammy could hear a note of surprise in his voice.

'It's about Alfie that we came.' From the tone of his voice, Sammy could tell that Joey had turned towards Tom. 'You was asking us about a man with a missing finger and we said that none of the clowns had a missing finger. But then we thought of someone after you had gone.'

'But he doesn't work in the Covent Garden Theatre,' said Lucky.

'No, and he isn't a real clown, neither.'

They were acting as if they were on a stage, thought Sammy. Clowns had a patter like this – just like tossing a ball, one to the other.

By the sounds the two clowns were doing a little dance. Mutsy gave a small, sharp bark, more like a laugh than a real bark.

'But he was the leader of them all!' sang the two clowns.

'Where would I find him? What's his name?' Tom's voice was sharp with anxiety.

'Hang on, Tom. Sit down a minute. Let the gentlemen finish telling us about this fellow,' said Jack.

There was a silence. When it came to it, the two clowns seemed reluctant to give more information about this mysterious man. Sammy decided to intervene.

'My brother Alfie is in Newgate prison,' he said, turning his face towards where he thought the clowns were sitting. He waited for a minute. Suddenly he had a huge lump in his throat. 'He might . . .' Now he had to force himself with all of his strong will, but the words had to be said. 'He might hang, unless you help us.'

Neither answered. Sammy could sense them looking at each other.

'Why would he do a thing like that, Lucky?' Joey's voice was puzzled.

Sammy held his breath.

'Don't know, Joey. Why would he murder Harry Booth?'

'If he's the one with the missing finger, well, he was the one that set the Scotland Yard on to Alfie. He bought me a pie and I told him where Alfie was.' Tom gulped and Sammy felt sorry for him. It must be hard for Tom to keep on telling the terrible thing that he had done.

'Must be him, mustn't it, Lucky?'

'But why? Not a nice fellow, but why murder?'

'And him from Drury Lane Theatre. Why murder an actor in the other place?'

'Drury Lane. He was from Drury Lane? What's his name?' Tom was on fire with impatience.

'That's right, sonny. He's the manager there.' There was a pause and then Joey seemed to make up his mind as he said quickly. 'His name is Fred White. I've never seen his fingers myself, but I did hear a rumour that he's missing a finger and that's why he always wears gloves.'

'Would you have noticed him there, that night? If he was dressed as a clown, would you have recognised him?' asked Sammy.

'We wasn't there that night, was we? We got taken on the same time as your brother, after the murder.

But you know who might know? Rosa. She could have been there. Nice girl, Rosa. You might have a word with her.'

'Where would he have got the outfit?' asked Sammy. 'Wouldn't someone at Covent Garden Theatre have to give him the clothes, make up his face – that sort of thing?'

'No way,' said Joey with a laugh. 'We clowns, we all have our own outfits. Every man is different. They're our trademark – we all do our own make-up, too. We're supposed to arrive dressed up at the theatre. Managers like that. It gives a bit of free advertising. Whips up a bit of interest.'

'So,' said Tom slowly, 'Fred White would have had to find his own costume.'

At these words, the two clowns jumped up, clapped their hands in an exaggerated way, each turned a somersault and then sat down again, turning their smiling, painted faces towards Tom. Mutsy gave a quick bark and wagged his tail in appreciation.

Life was a game to them, Tom supposed. But the information that they had given was of deadly serious consequence to Alfie. He thought about it for a few minutes and knew what he had to do.

Tom's voice was determined as he said, 'I'm going

to get that costume. If we can find someone at Covent Garden to remember it, we'll prove that Fred White was there that night.'

'And Sarah might go and see Inspector Grey – and tell him that she has found the name of the man with three fingers,' said Jack.

'And then we'll be on the way to proving that Alfie is innocent,' continued Tom. He paused for a moment and when he spoke again it was in a quiet low voice. 'I'll get that costume if it's the last thing I do.'

CHAPTER 27

TOM'S QUEST

There was nothing more boring than watching a play in a half-empty, silent theatre, thought Tom. He had got in easily enough to Drury Lane Theatre, had used some of their precious pence to buy a standing-only ticket for the pit. He had hardly noticed the performance. There were no clowns, there was hardly anyone in the boxes and the stalls were half-empty. No laughs, no shouts. It was all very dull.

'Had lions and tigers a few months ago,' said a hoarse man standing beside him. 'Drew big crowds, but not enough to pay for them. I've heard that the manager still owes the circus people for them. If he don't pay soon, they say he'll go bankrupt. He don't know what to do or where to turn; that's what they say.'

'Is that a fact?' said Tom, storing up the conversation in his mind. Could that be why the manager of Drury Lane wanted to start a riot in the Covent Garden Theatre? Did he want to stop people going there in the hopes that they would come to his theatre instead? But why was Harry Booth murdered? Perhaps Alfie could find a reason for that.

And then he shook himself. It was no good relying on Alfie to solve this puzzle. Alfie was in Newgate behind bars. The gang would have to do without him. It's up to me now, thought Tom. He pushed the information about the manager of Drury Lane to the back of his mind and began to wonder where he could hide when the performance eventually finished.

'That's right,' the hoarse man continued to whisper in Tom's ear. 'They say that the ghost of Charles Macklin has been seen every night and that's a sign of doom.'

Tom stirred uneasily. He didn't like ghosts. When he was younger, Alfie used to amuse himself by pretending to be a howling phantom and Tom had never managed to get away from the feeling of panic at the thought of seeing a ghost.

He tried not to listen as the man poured into his ear the story of a bad-tempered actor called Charles Macklin who had killed a fellow actor. And then, luckily, the final curtain was dropped and the actors came on stage in a long line.

'Where's the manager's office then so that I can ask for me money back?' asked Tom, inwardly congratulating himself on his cleverness. He had intended asking someone how to find the office and now this had come up quite naturally.

'Down by the ticket office,' said his new friend. 'You thinking of going in there? I wouldn't, if I were you. That Fred White, he's a funny man.'

'Funny man?' Tom asked quickly as they both prepared to move off with the rest of the people in the standing section of the pit.

'I've heard that he's bad-tempered.'

Tom clapped his hand to his pocket. 'Lost me handkerchief,' he said. 'I'd better have a look.'

'Probably a pickpocket, always keep me hands in me pocket myself.' The man didn't even turn his head after Tom who was by now crawling around on the floor, looking under the seats to the side of where they had been standing.

After a minute, he stayed very still. The theatre was

emptying fast. The musicians had climbed out of their orchestra pit and had gone along the aisle, chatting to each other. The place would not be cleaned until the morning; Tom knew that from what Sarah had said about Covent Garden.

He waited and stayed hidden. A man came down the aisle – Tom could hear his boots – and shouted 'Anyone there?' a couple of times and switched off the limelights at the front of the stage.

I'll wait until the other lights are switched off, thought Tom.

It seemed ages before the lamplighter man came clumping down – the side aisle this time. Tom dared not look, but after a few minutes he could see the long, black shadow on the floor near to the stage begin to spread. The lights were being extinguished one by one and the darkness was growing minute by minute.

And then suddenly Tom knew that something was going to happen that would give away his hiding place. The dust under the seats filled his mouth and nose with fine particles and the impulse to sneeze grew and grew. He held his nose firmly and tried to take in shallow breaths through his mouth. His face swelled, his head hurt and his ears felt as if they would pop off from the side of his head. Perhaps he could just give a tiny sneeze, he thought, just something that would relieve the pressure, but he knew that would be impossible. The force that built up inside him was too vast – only a thunderous sneeze would relieve it.

'That's the lot, then,' came a shout after a time that seemed endless to Tom. He peeped out cautiously. The man carried a lantern and his black shadow was coming up the aisle on the far side of the theatre.

Give him a minute to get clear, thought Tom.

The lamplighter shut the door with a bang. Tom sat up and knew that he could not hold in the sneeze any longer. Just a small one, he thought, but the sneeze burst out with an enormous crack and it filled the whole theatre with the noise of its explosion. Tom crouched down again, certain that a sound like that would be heard outside. He waited, heart thudding for a few minutes, but still all was quiet and dark.

Now he could get on with the job that he had come to do. He counted up to twenty in his mind and then eased himself out from under the seat and stood up. The darkness was complete. Not the slightest glimmer of street gas lamps came through the heavy curtains. There was something almost frightening about this darkness, almost as though heavy, smothering soot was weighing down on him. He edged his way along the row, keeping his hand on the backs of the seats in the row in front of him.

And then he had reached the end of the row. He must be in the middle aisle. He stepped out and became instantly disorientated, turning round and round and trying to grab something solid, something to hang on to. Tom had never experienced such blackness before – London streets were lit during the hours of darkness and their cellar always had a glimmer of light coming down from the gas light outside. Desperately, he got down on his knees, his right hand flailing around until it hit something solid.

It was a seat. He felt it very carefully, checking the position of the chair back before moving up the aisle. He resolved to take everything very slowly – there might still be people outside and if he tripped and fell he would alert them to his presence. Step by step he moved in a careful shuffle and thought of Sammy who went striding out into a blackness like this every day of his life.

Now, there was nothing left. No chair back as he stretched out his hand. For a moment he thought he had become disorientated again, but then he realised that he must have come to the end of the row and there would be a wide space of about six foot before he reached the door. He felt silly and cowardly, but he got down on his hands and knees and crawled towards the door. Once he felt its solid panels, he stood up, his heart beating hard with excitement and fumbled for the door knob.

He found it easily enough. He found it and turned it. Pushed. Then pulled. Turned again. Pulled and pushed again. But nothing worked. He had known the truth in the first moment. The door had been locked.

He would have to stay here until morning.

CHAPTER 28

DEADLY PERIL

'Terrible smell of gas in here! Someone should do something about it before we are all poisoned.'

The loud, cheerful voice woke Tom. A ray of light slanted down the middle aisle. Alarmed, he rolled back under the seat. He should have gone further down! This row was only second from the top and if anyone investigated he would be easily found. He had a splitting headache and he felt slightly sick. It had been a terrible night; he turned his thoughts away from the nightmares that had plagued him with visions of a one-eyed ghost.

'Have a word with the management, old chap,' said

another voice. 'I'm sure you'll get a good hearing. Go and see the manager. He's sitting in his office, groaning over his accounts. I'm sure that he would be delighted to have a little chat about the expense of getting the gas pipes looked at.'

Both of them laughed cheerfully and then went off, leaving the door standing invitingly open.

I have to do it, Tom told himself when they had gone. He stood up cautiously. No one was around. He needed to get out of the pit, go towards the entrance door, lurk there until the manager came out of his office, pop in, search his cupboard for clues.

But it all seemed impossible now!

It would be better just to slip out and go home before he got himself into any trouble.

Another night imprisoned in that darkness would kill him, he thought.

And then he thought of Alfie, and of Newgate prison and knew that he could not walk away.

Suddenly he saw it. The perfect disguise.

Leaning against the wall, next to the door, was a broom and below it a small dustpan and brush. Tom, with one final look around, slipped over, seized the broom and started to sweep.

Just out in the passageway at first. Take it easy –

don't rush, he told himself. Then a trip to the large rubbish bin outside the back entrance. Empty the dustpan. Go back. Then a bit further up the passageway. More busy sweeping. And then the ticket desk came in sight. Someone was sitting there.

A well-dressed gentleman came in and approached the man in the ticket office. Tom moved a little closer, still busily sweeping. No one seemed interested in this ragged boy working away.

'Any possibility of a box? We'll be a party of six.'

'Just a minute, sir. I'll have a word with the manager.'

A small, fat man appeared. So this must be Fred White, manager of Drury Lane Theatre. Tom shuddered, remembering how the same small, fat man had bought him a pie at Smithfield. He kept his head well down and moved back into the shadows. Important people like managers seldom bothered looking at servants with brooms, he knew. All the same, he was relieved when the man's eyes did not turn in his direction.

What he needed now was to find the clown's costume and to see whether anyone who was backstage on the night of Harry Booth's murder remembered a clown dressed like that. A clown who had no business to be there at Covent Garden Theatre.

Unless he was up to something.

'I'd like to inspect the boxes if that's possible. I want to choose one with a very good view of the stage,' the gentleman repeated to the manager.

The opportunity might be coming. Tom gripped his broom so tightly that the wood dug into his palm.

'Just come with me, sir. We have quite few boxes on offer for Saturday night. You can take your pick.'

'All right if I sweep in the manager's office while he's out of the way?' Tom asked the man in the box office. It was taking a chance, but if it came off it would be worth it.

'Be quick, then.' The man hardly lifted his eyes from his work.

Tom was quick, very quick. In a second he was through the door and looking around eagerly.

No cupboard anywhere in the room.

Just shelves and one bookcase.

A desk – not there, the drawers would be too shallow to hold a costume.

Not behind the door – his cloak hung there.

But no top hat. Where did he put his top hat? Everyone wore a top hat in the street.

Two doors in the room . . .

Leaving his broom leaning against the desk, Tom turned the handle of the second door.

It did not lead to a corridor, but to a huge, walk-in cupboard. The top hat was on a shelf there. Beneath it hung a few spare shirts, and a glossy black frock coat. Nothing else was in the cupboard except a large locked case. Tom tried to force the lock open, but it was no good. The case was old but the lock was sturdy. Tom went quietly to the door and looked out. There was no sign of the manager coming back. Quickly he went to the desk. Would there be anything there to help him?

Immediately he found what he was looking for. On the desk lay an envelope and stuck into the flap of the envelope was a long, thin knife. The manager must have been slitting it when he was called to the booking desk.

Tom slipped out the knife and went back to the cupboard. His hands shook. Would he be able to do this in time? Quickly he inserted the knife into the lock on the case. One of Maggie the Plucker's gang had taught him how to do this. For a moment he thought it would not work and then suddenly there was a click. One of the locks snapped open.

And then loud footsteps sounded in the corridor.

The manager was coming back. Quickly and silently Tom pulled the door shut. He moved soundlessly behind the frock coat. If anyone came in and shone a light he was sunk, but still it was worth a try. The man might just take his hat from the top shelf, finding it by touch and by long habit.

But he was in luck. The door to the cupboard did not open. A drawer was slammed shut and then another. And then a voice raised. He was shouting something to the box office clerk. There was no answer. The manager shouted again. Still no answer.

'Deaf fool,' he muttered and then left the room in a hurry, slamming the door shut after him.

Tom acted quickly. One second to open the door a little and allow some light in, another second to insert the knife into the second lock.

Nothing happened.

Try again. He heard the words in his mind and they steadied him. Funnily enough they were spoken with Sammy's voice.

Lightly and almost carelessly he inserted the knife into the lock once more and this time it worked.

And there was a clown's costume – in black and white with a frilly-sleeved shirt and frills on the ends of the pantaloons. Beside it was a tall, cone-shaped clown's hat and an orange wig. Tom picked up the frilly-sleeved shirt. The frills were edged with orange fur to match the wig. With trembling hands, he stuffed the shirt under his jacket.

Replacing everything else as carefully as he could, Tom left the office and returned to the corridor. Quickly he dumped the broom and picked up the dustpan.

'Just going to find the bin,' he muttered to the man at the desk and flew down the steps, abandoning the dustpan at the bottom of them.

The frilly shirt fell out as he bent over, but he picked it up in a flash and this time he squeezed the muddy garment into his pocket.

It would be a mess, but perhaps he could rinse it under the Broad Street pump.

The important thing was to keep the shirt safe until Joey and Lucky got a chance to show it around. That muddy, crumpled piece of material might be able to save Alfie's life.

In his mind was a picture of the gallows outside Newgate prison.

Only two more days to go.

CHAPTER 29

THE TRIAL

The courtroom of the Old Bailey seemed to be filled from floor to ceiling with faces – strange, oval shapes that glistened white in the flaring light of the gas lamps.

The noise in that place was terrible. Alfie stopped for a moment when he met the solid wall of sound and had to be pushed on by the warder who dealt him a savage blow in the small of the back and made him stumble. Roars, shouts, moans, laughs – how could anyone laugh in a place that gave out such savage sentences – in a place that meant death for some and a life-in-death for others?

Alfie was pushed into the wooden dock, heard the door slam shut behind him and looked out at the scene, at all the faces and then he turned away, sickened. He stared down at the wooden floor of the dock where he stood, looked at the walls that caged him in, looked at his manacled hands and his shackled legs. Anywhere, except at that inhuman crowd. He clutched the wooden sides of the dock and tried to stiffen his knees. He hoped that no one was near enough to see how he trembled. Suddenly he thought of his grandfather who had a great belief in Heaven – who thought that the minute you died you shot straight up through the blue sky to this unknown place where no one was ever hungry, thirsty or cold. Was it true? Alfie hoped so.

The jury were to one side of him, twelve men sitting on cushioned seats behind a glass screen in their own box. They looked at him suspiciously – almost as though he had already been found guilty and they were just waiting for sentence to be passed. Alfie raised his head and straightened his back. The boy before him, who had been sentenced to transportation for fourteen years, had been carried out screaming and calling for his mother. Alfie was determined that he wasn't going to do that.

'All rise!' yelled a court official and most people stood up, though many in the gallery above did not bother.

The judge came in, his long robes sweeping the floor behind him, the coarse white hair of his wig hanging on either side of his long face. He didn't look at Alfie, but climbed the steps, seated himself and arranged his mantle around him – a dark red mantle, the colour of old blood. The usher seemed about to call for silence again, but the judge opened his mouth and all the noise died down as people leant forward to hear what he was going to say about this new case.

'There has seldom been a more heinous crime,' said the judge with emphasis. Alfie was not too sure what he meant by 'heinous', but he guessed by the shocked faces of the lawyers on the benches in front of him that it was pretty bad.

He had no lawyer to defend him. The turnkey had told him cheerfully that he didn't stand a chance without a lawyer.

'*All the world's a stage*, as the great William Shakespeare observed, but few people meet their death on a real stage,' said the judge, looking hard at Alfie. He seemed to be very keen on this chap Shakespeare, as the next few sentences were all about him as well, but then he got on to Harry Booth. He seemed to be very upset about the fact that Harry Booth actually snuffed it on the stage in front of the Queen, instead of being knifed down a dark alley at night, or strangled with a wire and his body thrown into the river at dawn.

Then the judge sat back, nodded to one of the bewigged lawyers and said, 'Yes, Mr Witherington.'

Mr Witherington rose and gave the judge an elegant bow, before throwing his gown back over his shoulders and sticking his thumbs under his armpits.

'Gentlemen of the jury,' he said solemnly. 'As you would expect, Scotland Yard have been tireless in their endeavours to catch the man or men who planned this terrible murder.' He paused for a moment and then said dramatically, 'Unfortunately, because of the obdurate obstinacy of a boy, that boy whom you see before you, gentlemen of the jury, they have not been able to make any more arrests.' He paused again and then continued. 'So, shall Harry Booth go to his grave unavenged? Gentlemen of the jury, I put it to you that Heaven, itself, would cry out for vengeance if no one pays the penalty for his murder.'

And then all of the jury turned their faces towards Alfie and he read his fate in their accusing eyes.

'This boy,' Mr Witherington was saying, 'was

central to the plan. You could say, gentlemen of the jury, that he was the lynch-pin, that he was the —'

'Mr Witherington,' interrupted the judge, 'get on with the case.'

Probably wanted to get home for his dinner, thought Alfie. His life was at stake, and the judge just wanted this case over and done with quickly!

'Yes, m'lud,' said Mr Witherington obediently and went on to explain to the jury how Alfie came up through the trapdoor to divert the attention of Harry Booth and of the audience while poison was being poured into the glass. Alfie half-listened. Inspector Cutting from Scotland Yard had said all of these things many times to him and he had denied it until he was weary.

Alfie had considered inventing a gang for them – a vicious, brutal leader who had bullied and beaten a poor innocent boy like himself until he did their bidding. However, he realised that he would do himself little good by a story like this. He had enough sense to know that nothing would satisfy them but to lay their hands on a man who could be hanged for murder.

And failing that, a boy would have to do.

CHAPTER 30

THE WITNESSES

'Any witness to good character?' The judge sounded bored and contemptuous.

'Yes, sir.' Alfie's voice was low and husky. He cleared his throat.

The warder standing behind him gave him another savage poke in the back. 'Say, my lord,' he whispered loudly.

'Yes, my lord,' echoed Alfie. 'I have a witness to good character.' For a moment he panicked in case the judge would pretend not to hear him. This was probably his last chance. The message from Sarah had just come to him last night. It was a short note and just said, *Ask for a witness to good character.*

'Witness of character of the prisoner, Alfie Sykes, accused of murder,' bawled the usher, going to the door and raising his voice as if he was endeavouring to alert the whole population of London.

Just one man entered, though. A neat, small man with dark eyes and bushy eyebrows. He gave a piece of paper – his name, thought Alfie – to the usher and then went into the witness box and laid his hand on the bible, swearing to tell the truth, the whole truth and nothing but the truth. Inspector Denham looked quite at home, thought Alfie.

'My lord, I can bear witness to the good character of this boy, Alfie Sykes. He is an orphan.'

'They all are, Inspector, they all are,' said the judge and his joke made the whole court laugh. Mr Witherington almost doubled up, he was so amused. Alfie's heart sank.

'He lives in Bow Street near to my police station and cares for his blind brother and his two cousins,' continued Inspector Denham as the laughter died away. He didn't seem bothered by it. He looked directly at the judge as he said with emphasis, 'He has never been in trouble with the police – on the contrary he has been of assistance on many occasions.'

The judge, Alfie was thankful to see, did not make a joke out of this. In fact, he looked sharply at the Bow Street inspector as if he were interested in that statement. It was a slight exaggeration, of course, to say that he had never been in trouble with the police, but Alfie supposed that you could say he had never been in bad trouble.

'I am very glad to have the occasion to give this evidence,' continued Inspector Denham. 'Could I beg your ludship's indulgence to present a few facts about this boy and the terrible murder? Facts,' he added quickly as the judge opened his mouth, 'which have only just come to my notice.'

'Go ahead, Inspector.' The judge sounded weary. He cast another quick glance at the clock. Alfie's heart sank again.

'The boy's story, that he saw a hand wearing the frilly sleeve of a clown, come out from behind the curtain holding a phial and just rushed on stage to warn Harry Booth, has been disbelieved,' said Inspector Denham in dry tones. 'I have waiting outside a witness who is prepared to swear that this clown's shirt . . .'

Inspector Denham broke off, turned around, picked up the brown paper parcel from the bench behind him, gave one look at the court and began slowly to unwrap it. The crowd in the gallery stood up. Those in front craned their necks over the rails and those at the back started to shout: 'Siddown! Hats off! Hold it up, Bobby!' Suddenly the whole court was in uproar.

The judge looked annoyed, the usher shouted for silence, the lawyers stopped yawning and whispering to each other behind their hands and some of them stood up also. Now there were shouts of 'Hurry up! Wottcher doing?'

Inspector Denham was purposely dragging out the moment, thought Alfie, looking at him with sharpened interest. He watched in astonishment as Inspector Denham took out of his brown paper parcel a frilly clown shirt and explained to the judge that it belonged to a man that had no business to be in Covent Garden Theatre that night. Alfie's breath quickened. Had someone been investigating on his behalf?

At that moment there was a huge laugh from the gallery and then a rustling movement. Alfie, looking up, saw that all heads had turned away from the scene below and were looking back at the door behind them. The crowd opened up and stood back as ten clowns, walking in pairs, came through the door and trooped down until they reached the rail. They squatted down there, the tall hats and white, painted faces just peering over the rail.

'I ask your ludship's permission to call a witness to this,' said Inspector Denham politely.

The judge nodded and then snapped something at the usher, who was gazing at the clowns in the gallery with an expression of stupefaction.

The next witness was a surprise to Alfie. Sarah, watching from the gallery above, could see that he had an astonished look on his face. Of course, he would, like herself, have hardly noticed Rosa on that night at Covent Garden Theatre. In any case, Rosa was not dressed like an actress now, but wore a neat brown dress with a high neck and a plain white collar– all borrowed from the costume cupboard at the theatre. She had coiled and netted her exuberant golden curls into a demure knot at the back of her neck and carried a respectable-looking brown silk umbrella. She curtsied politely to the judge, was bowed into the witness box by Inspector Denham, laid her hand delicately on the Bible and swore to tell the whole truth and nothing but the truth in a low, gentle voice, which nevertheless carried well. It was, thought Sarah, a great performance.

'Your witness, Mr Witherington,' said Inspector

Denham, quite at home in the Old Bailey courthouse. He whispered something to Rosa, handed the shirt to her and then stepped back, standing at the side and watching intently.

'I was present backstage in Covent Garden Theatre on the night when Harry Booth was murdered,' said Rosa in refined, young-lady-like tones. 'I was . . . was adjusting my costume when I heard a click from the door at the back. It's always kept locked during performances and the key was missing that day. But now a clown came in with the missing key in his hand. I looked at him carefully because I thought all of the clowns were already there. He was wearing an orange wig, and he had orange fur to match the wig on the ends of the sleeves. He was wearing this shirt.' Dramatically she held up the shirt with its orange trimmings. 'And then I counted and saw that there were eleven clowns instead of ten.'

The judge frowned and looked at Mr Witherington who rose to his feet.

'Permission to cross-examine, m'lud,' he said. Without waiting, he swung around and addressed Rosa angrily. 'Is this some lie you've made up?' he roared. 'Are you an accomplice to that lad in the dock?'

Rosa gave him a stunned glance and then burst into

tears. Or at least she held a lace handkerchief to her eyes, sobbed delicately and averted her head. Although Sarah was shaking with nerves she felt herself smile. Rosa could always cry to order. She was a born actress.

'Mr Witherington!' protested the judge. 'Moderate your language, please. You are upsetting the young lady.'

'Sorry, m'lud,' Mr Witherington seemed a little uncertain, but then he tried a new approach.

'How do we know you are telling the truth?' he asked, trying to make his voice sound gentle.

'Because Mr John Osborne, the stagehand, was up on a ladder fixing one of the curtain rings and he saw the clown, also,' said Rosa sweetly. 'He will tell you that I am speaking the truth.'

Sarah held her breath. It had taken all of Rosa's skills to persuade John Osborne to give evidence. She clenched her hands. Would he be there? And if not, would Rosa's evidence be useless?

'M'lud, the police would like to call John Osborne to give evidence, if you have finished with this young lady,' said Inspector Denham.

'Call John Osborne!'

And he was there with his ruined face and his beautiful voice. And he told the same story. But would it be enough?

John Osborne was not as good a witness as Rosa. He kept getting flustered and allowing the lawyer to upset him.

The time was going on. Several times Alfie saw the judge's eyes go to the clock. It looked as though he was keen to finish the case and pass sentence.

And then there was a sudden commotion outside. A voice, loudly raised. The clashing of iron shackles. A sharp knock on the door. The usher went to the door. Mr Witherington forgot where he was in the middle of a question and just stood staring. The people in the gallery stood up. Inspector Denham gave a smile of satisfaction and stopped watching the clock. The judge looked furious and scowled at the usher whose creaking boots tiptoed up the steps and stopped as he reached up to whisper in his lordship's ear.

'What!'

There had been a sudden silence and the judge's one word rang like a pistol shot through the room.

More whispers from the usher, strained attention from the gallery, the lawyers whispered together, Inspector Denham studied his boots, Rosa smiled her sweet, gentle smile, and Alfie looked from one to the other with sharpened interest.

'Admit the gentlemen from Scotland Yard and their witness,' said the Judge.

And in came Inspector Grey, and behind him, flanked by two policemen, a small round man, his shackles clanking on the stone floor.

Inspector Grey had a glass phial held upright between finger and thumb. Alfie recognised it as soon as he saw it, but then . . .

The gas lamp above the entrance flared up in the sudden draught. The light shone down upon the man and illuminated his manacled hands. He held them out stiffly in front of him.

One finger was missing from the right hand.

CHAPTER 31

CHINESE
LANTERNS

'Well, I'm blessed! Same old foggy London!' Alfie made his voice as casual as possible. He gripped Sammy's arm hard and grinned across at Sarah. She wasn't looking at him, though. Both she and Jack were looking over their shoulders.

'Where's Tom?' began Alfie. 'Is . . .' and then he stopped. The loud toot-toot of a tin whistle sounded and a group of clowns came out from the Old Bailey. They formed two lines, led by Joey and Lucky, walking on either side of Alfie and his gang.

'There's ten of them, no – eleven, counting the chap playing the music, and they're all dressed up in their

clowns' outfits and they're waving little flags.' Alfie
found that explaining things to Sammy helped him to
feel less embarrassed. He was still reeling from the
shock of the sudden release.

Sarah was pouring into his ear all the details of how
Joey the Clown had remembered that the manager of
Drury Lane Theatre, Fred White, was rumoured to
have three fingers. And how Tom, with great bravery
had spent the night in the theatre and had managed to
find and steal the shirt of the clown's outfit.

'And when Rosa saw the clown's outfit that Fred
White had been wearing, she remembered seeing it on
one of the clowns backstage on the night of the
murder,' Sarah went on. 'We all talked it over and
worked out that Fred White was causing riots just to
bankrupt Covent Garden Theatre so that his own
theatre would sell more tickets. Harry Booth found
out and blackmailed him. So Fred White murdered
Harry Booth!'

'And I had a chat with Inspector Denham,' put in
Sammy. 'He took a cab to Scotland Yard, immediately.'

Alfie had thought he would be interested in all this,
but now he found that he didn't really want to know.
Not now. Not when all his worst fears were so fresh in
his mind. He hoped no one would ask him questions,

either. He didn't want to talk about Newgate, above all he didn't want to think about Newgate. So, though he had a voice like a crow, he joined in lustily when the clowns began to sing and even took a few dancing steps in imitation of the clowns.

And then like a bolt of lightning, Mutsy tore down the Strand, threading his way through the crowds, and hurled himself against Alfie, almost knocking him to the ground. Alfie went down on his knees and hugged his dog, holding the massive paw, stroking the domed head, putting his cheek against the rough coat. He said nothing but breathed in deeply, and the pungent smell of wet dog seemed to blot out the stinks of Newgate. He looked up into Tom's embarrassed face. His cousin didn't know what to say and Alfie sought quickly for some joke, but could think of nothing and buried his head in Mutsy again.

'Come on then, young shaver, no lagging allowed here!' shouted Lucky, and all the clowns laughed in that strange, high-pitched tee-hee style of clowns.

'Who are you calling an old lag? I've only been in prison once,' roared Alfie. He carefully placed Sammy's hand in Jack's and then began to dance, darting in and out of the clowns and imitating their tricks. He took no notice of the people staring. He heard someone talking about him. One of the clowns was explaining to a man in a black coat that Alfie had just been freed from Newgate, that he had been wrongfully accused of murder.

'Newgate?' The man took out a small notebook from his pocket. 'What was that like, sonny? I'd like to interview you if you'll give me a few minutes of your time. My name is Charles Dickens. I write for the newspapers.'

Suddenly Alfie felt dizzy. The lights from the street gas lamps danced up and down in front of his eyes. He put out his hand, fumbling for something to hold on to and found his wrist grabbed.

'Hallo, hallo, hallo,' said Joey's voice. 'Now then, my old covey, stick your snifter into this flower of mine. Have you ever smelled anything more bootilacious?'

Alfie swallowed hard, but obediently moved his nose towards the cabbage-sized cloth flower that Joey wore in his buttonhole. The next moment he started back, a stream of water running down his face. All the clowns laughed in their usual high-pitched 'Tee-hee-hee'.

Alfie blinked, wiped his face and laughed. The shock of the water had revived him.

'How did you do that trick?' he asked. But then he

forgot about his question. Mutsy, once he had got over his joy at Alfie's reappearance, had immediately made a beeline for the clown just in front of him. Now he just stood there, sniffing the man's pocket and wagging his tail.

The clown put his hand in his pocket. Alfie watched carefully. He expected another trick – a jack-in-the-box, or something like that, but the clown took out a tiny white dog, who immediately began to walk around the pavement on his back legs. The clown placed a miniature pointed hat on the dog's head. Mutsy stared at him in amazement and then began to wag his huge tail.

'Well, what have you got to say for yourself, Toby?' asked Alfie, stroking the little dog. 'You was the one that nabbed me, wasn't you?'

'Very sorry! Very, very sorry! Didn't knowed them jacks wanted to top you!' answered the dog Toby in a tiny voice.

'How did you do that?' screamed Tom, looking from the clown to the little dog, still trotting around on his back legs. 'Sammy, the voice just came right out of the little dog's mouth. Can he really speak, Mister?'

'Bless my soul,' squeaked Toby, 'I was born able to talk!'

'Wish I could learn to do that,' said Alfie, gazing enviously at the clown. He had seen ventriloquists with their dummies before now – there was one that used to do a routine on the steps of St Paul's church at Covent Garden, but having a real live dog as a dummy was so much better.

'Look at Mutsy,' said Sarah.

Mutsy was sitting in the middle of the pavement, staring at the little dog with a look of astonishment on his face.

The passers-by stopped to look and began to laugh at Toby's performance, especially when, slowly and carefully, Mutsy minced around just an inch behind the tiny dog, carefully sniffing him as the little dog danced along the pavement. Some people started to clap and more coins were dropped into Jack's cap, which he had hastily snatched off his head and held out.

Well, thought Alfie, that will pay for the rent this week and hopefully there will be something left over for sausages and some small beer when we get home.

And then he just concentrated on enjoying himself, on copying the clowns, getting in their way, falling over in an exaggerated manner, singing in his tuneless voice.

It all passed so quickly that he was astonished when they turned into Bow Street.

It was getting dark now and the lamplighter was holding his flame up to the little gas jets overheard. It was slow work, going from lamp to lamp and he had still not got as far as the cellar where the boys lived. That end of the street was dark.

But the pavement in front of their home was lit up.

An orange light burnt from behind the iron railings.

Alfie sprang forward, the song dying on his lips. He raced ahead, down the steps. The door was not locked. He pushed it open.

The dark damp cellar shimmered with light. It looked like Piccadilly Circus! There were candles everywhere and from the beam crossing above their heads a set of Chinese lanterns glowed in orange, blue, red and green. The fire blazed, the flames leaping up and making the cellar as warm as midsummer's day. Rosa was standing there, laughing as Mutsy licked her hand, his tail wagging and an amused look on his intelligent face.

There was a board in the centre of the cellar, propped up on a couple of stools and it was covered in food; with a large cake from the pastry cook's shop sitting in the centre of everything.

The one chair in the cellar was placed at the top of the board. On its back it had the shape of a garland cut out of cardboard, decorated with paper leaves.

In large unsteady letters around the garland was written: *WELCOME HOME, ALFIE.*

THE LONDON MURDER MYSTERIES

piccadillypress.co.uk/
londonmurdermysteries

Head online to find out more
about Alfie's world!

ACKNOWLEDGEMENTS

These London Murder Mysteries owe much to a man who was born almost two hundred years ago. I first read Charles Dickens at the age of seven – probably skipped large chunks – but I loved his characters and loved his descriptions of London. During the whole of a childhood spent in and out of hospital (never well enough to go to school until I was over fifteen), I educated myself by reading through a library of Victorian authors – but loved none as much as I loved Dickens.

Alfie and his gang came to life because of Charles Dickens and I am proud to acknowledge my debt. But inspiration is only the first step towards writing a book. For the successful conclusion of the process, I owe much to my family for all their help and support; to Peter Buckman, my agent for his sage advice; to Anne Clark, my wonderful editor, for her unremitting hard work, flashes of inspiration and determination not to let even the tiniest error escape her eagle eye. Thanks, Anne; it's a pleasure to work with you.

THE LONDON MURDER MYSTERIES

THE MONTGOMERY MURDER

The police must move fast to catch the killer of wealthy Mr Montgomery. They need an insider, someone streetwise, cunning, bold . . . someone like Alfie. When Inspector Denham makes him an offer, Alfie and his gang must sift clues, shadow suspects and negotiate a sinister world of double-dealing and danger.

THE DEADLY FIRE

A man's body lies in the burned-out wreckage of the Ragged School.
The police say the fire was just an accident – but Alfie suspects foul play.
Determined to find out the truth, Alfie and his gang must follow up each clue, investigate every suspect and risk their lives on the dangerous streets of Victorian London – until the ruthless murderer is caught.

THE LONDON MURDER MYSTERIES

DEATH OF A CHIMNEY SWEEP

Alfie knew who it was the moment he saw
the body under the gas lamp.
Joe the chimney sweep.
No one else seems to care about the death of a poor
boy, but Alfie has reason to believe that Joe was
murdered. So he and his gang will risk their lives on
the rooftops of London and brave the dark,
dangerous world of the chimney sweeps,
until they uncover the deadly truth.

COMING JULY 2011

SAXBY SMART
PRIVATE DETECTIVE
SIMON CHESHIRE

Be the sleuth yourself and crack all the cases!

In each story Saxby Smart – schoolboy detective – gives you, the reader, clues which help solve the mystery. Are you 'smart' enough to find the answers?

The **Curse** of the **Ancient Mask**

A mysterious curse, suspicious sabotage of a school competition, and a very unpleasant relative all conspire to puzzle Saxby Smart, schoolboy private detective.
Stories include: *The Curse of the Ancient Mask*, *The Mark of the Purple Homework* and *The Clasp of Doom*.

The Hangman's Lair

A terrifying visit to the Hangman's Lair to recover stolen money, a serious threat of blackmail, and a mystery surrounding a stranger's unearthly powers test Saxby to the limit in this set of case files!
Stories include: *The Hangman's Lair*, *Diary of Fear* and *Whispers from the Dead*.